Raid
Rise Of Mankind Book 3

John Walker

DISCLAIMER

This is a work of fiction. Names, characters, business, places, events, and incidents are either the products of the author's imagination or used in a fictitious manner. Any resemblance to actual persons, living or dead, or actual events is purely coincidental. This story contains explicit language and violence.

Blurb

Earth has nearly completed a second ship, a sister vessel
to the Behemoth. This crowning achievement is
hampered by a lack of a necessary element called Ulem,
mined in deep space in planetoids and asteroids spread
throughout Alliance space. The closest such station failed
to deliver their goods. A lone security guard managed to
deploy a distress call with a simple message: PIRATES
HAVE TAKEN THE STATION

Turning to the Earth military council, the Alliance asks
them to send the Behemoth to take back the station. In
return, they will provide them with all the Ulem they
need for two vessels and stay on to complete the
construction of the ships. But the Behemoth has just
finished a nasty engagement at a research facility and
has not even returned home yet.

Chances are good that the pirates are merely there to
steal an enormous amount of the expensive mineral but
you never know...

Prologue

The explosion left him dazed, knocking him to the floor. His body went numb and his limbs ignored every attempt to move. Terror clung to his heart as it suddenly dawned on him that he may've been blown to pieces. He thanked the fates when his fingers moved, causing his forearm to ache.

You have to get up and go!

Danger remained close. Whoever attacked the station might be close and they didn't seem like they wanted to take prisoners. If they found him wallowing in misery, he'd be done. If he planned on being of any use to his colleagues and friends, he needed to get somewhere safe. He might well be the only person capable of sending a distress call.

He just had to think of where to go. What part of the station might be safe enough to take a moment and send for help? His mind wouldn't work and he couldn't remember the security stations which had been drilled into his head by his superiors since he joined the station.

Of course, he'd been concussed so it made sense that he struggled to remember anything.

Pain lanced through him and part of him just wanted to give up. It would be so easy. Just close his eyes and wait for whoever attacked to find him, possibly ending his life. But he refused to give up. Some defiant aspect of his being demanded he stand, that he pull himself together but his limbs weren't quite ready for the exuberance yet.

As a result, he wondered about the situation and how it all came to pass. What had he been doing in the first place? How had he arrived at this situation? When he thought about the world around him and the explosion, he felt a moment of fear but there was more to it than mindless terror. Someone did this deliberately but who? And why?

Thirty minutes earlier, at the start of his shift, it was just another day. His mind wandered...

***

Ander left his quarters at the start of first shift, locked up and headed toward the security offices to check in. His weapon weighed heavily on his right side and he had to tighten his belt to keep it from slipping down. He wore his newest uniform and it felt stiff. The cleaner really did a number on it.

The promenade already bustled with activity as miners and their families went about their morning business. Operations tended to go around the clock but the Chief Operator called off all activity for two full shifts, roughly twelve hours. Ander figured he'd hear about it eventually, whether from his boss or through a public announcement.

A line at his favorite cafe made him groan. Under normal circumstances, he just walked up and picked up an order but with all the extra people there, every business was packed to the gills. He checked the time and figured he could afford to wait for a few minutes. The waitstaff hurried as much as they could.

When he finally got his turn, Tierna smiled as he approached. "Hello, Ander! How're you today?"

Tierna had been someone Ander wanted to ask out on a romantic date for a long time but never got up the nerve to do so. She was a pretty lady, someone he looked forward to seeing every morning when he got his drink. He'd come close to talking to her about getting together plenty of times but always backed out at the last moment.

That morning was no different. He tried to work up the courage and failed, instead opting to keep to his normal routine. He shrugged and finally replied. "A little tired. A little bored. You?"

"Busy! We don't normally get such a rush on first shift."

"I know what you mean," Ander replied, glancing over his shoulder. People began to cue up behind him. "Can I get a paragir smoothie?"

Tierna sucked air through her teeth, looking apologetic. "I'm afraid not. The last shipment of supplies only contained a half order. We ran out."

"Damn…" Ander hummed. "How about a torin blend?"

"That I've got. Just scan your card, please."

Ander complied and stepped aside for his drink, staring off into space. Others exhibited far less patience than he had, going so far as to rush the staff while bouncing on the balls of their feet. Many of them needed to get business done while they had the chance. Mining work tended to be hard, even with modern equipment. Those who did it took advantage of whatever time off they were afforded.

News played on a nearby monitor, a piece about the war effort. Ander ignored it until he heard about a potential new addition to the alliance. The Earth people finally were about to be admitted. It's about time, he thought. Anyone who gets attacked by those fiends should be admitted immediately. They shouldn't have to prove themselves worthy of survival.

Ander didn't always have the most liberal views but when it came to people's lives, he didn't like to compromise. It was one of the reasons he left the military and took up security work. While he served, he killed many of the enemies and it helped to ease his conscience some about giving back to his country. After seven years though, he needed a change of pace.

Yes, the mining facility could be boring but it held its own rewards. Whenever he broke up a disagreement or helped emergency response units save a life, he felt pride in his work. Few times in the military made him proud. Their operations tended to be harsh and final, rarely resulting in anyone being saved but themselves.

Fighting for one's life, even if it ultimately meant holding back a tide of invaders, didn't amount to the direct interactions he had on the mining station.

Ander grabbed his drink from the bar and waved to Tierna as he left. She smiled at him and returned to her job, looking a bit more harried than when he arrived. Depending on when the mines re-opened, every business on the promenade would have a busy day and the poor bastards who had to patrol it would have their work cut out for them.

The security offices were mostly empty. Everyone had to hit their beat fast to account for all the people milling about. Ander checked in at the computer console and looked over the duty roster. He'd been assigned to subsection six, a part of the station where few people ever went. It was a maintenance area but they'd received reports of suspicious activity.

Three days of patrolling hadn't turned up a thing. Ander would've thought it especially boring but for the fact it tended to be creepy. The noises down there of creaking metal chilled his blood, even though he'd spent a lot of time down there. His imagination made it scarier. In his mind's eye, the wall came free and he was casually sucked into space.

Whoever's been going down there for illegal activity has nerves of steel.

Ander never liked space travel all that much. He operated as a ground soldier, one who tended to put his boots on dirt. Boarding actions horrified him and travel between battle zones unnerved him. He'd mostly gotten over his phobia by the time he boarded the mining station but when he heard noises, the fear came back full force.

Oh well. There're survival suits down there. I'll be fine. I just have to believe that. I'll be fine.

Parin, his boss, waved to Ander as he prepared to go. "How's it going today?"

"Okay, I guess. When do I get out of this patrol duty? Did I make you angry or something?"

"What? Not at all!" Parin shook his head emphatically. "I trust your judgement down there. Some of the guys are a little young. We need a veteran down there if we catch anyone doing anything. Besides, I thought you'd like the peace and quiet."

Ander chuckled. "It's not quiet down there, sir. Believe me. But I get it. Can I...well...make a request?"

"Sure, what's up?"

"Will you put me on something else tomorrow? I don't want five days of that place in a row."

Parin nodded. "Done. Thanks for being flexible."

Ander left, trying to feel as cheery as Parin seemed to think he was. He had to take an elevator down to Subsection four then descend a ladder to get to his destination. That area tended to be a little on the cool side, which was about the only thing that suited Ander. The rest of the station tended to run hot and he rarely felt comfortable with his uniform jacket on.

On the second ladder down, the explosion tossed him the rest of the way down and he landed on his stomach. As his mind caught up to the present, he found the strength to stand and stumbled to the wall. He leaned against it and scanned the area, drawing his weapon. No one was around.

The station was attacked but that was probably a warning shot. The only reason I took so much punishment was because the shields are weaker down here. It made the whole place shake. What luck...I guess.

Shouts from above drew his attention but he knew they were mere echoes. The actual people speaking had to be nearer to the promenade. Did the station get boarded by hostiles or was Ander hearing the inhabitants freak out about the attack? The answer to the question would indicate whether Ander should join the people or stay out of sight long enough to help.

I think I'll err on the side of caution.

Ander plunged deeper into Subsection Six and entered the tiny security station. No one had used it in a long time. His own communicator worked just fine but now, he needed information he would only get from the computer system. He logged in and tapped his foot, waiting for the exterior camera to light up.

His eyes widened when an Alliance cruiser flickered on the screen. What the... A freighter moved in to dock, one Ander felt certain must be a pirate. They have a battleship!? How! A station wide message broadcast from central security telling the people to retreat to their homes while they attempted to repel boarders.

I'm not sure we have the muscle for repelling that much firepower, Ander thought. Especially if they decide to start blasting away.

A moment later, a message came through from the attackers. Ander clicked it on to listen.

"Citizens of Mining Station Sys Alpha," the man's voice sounded dispassionate but serious. "Your facility now belongs to us. Offer resistance and you'll all die. We can spend the next few days scraping up the goods through space. We know the codes to your computer systems and can lower your shields. Think about what that means for a minute."

Ander looked around frantically for inspiration on what he should do but nothing came to him. His own boss, Parin replied to them.

"We will not offer resistance if you assure us no one will be harmed."

"You're not in the position to demand anything," the pirate replied. "Surrender or die. Those are your choices. You have five seconds to decide."

"We surrender!" Parin shouted.

No! They're bluffing! They must be. These bastards don't want to scavenge up the goods, they want to load it up like they're a legal entity! Ander slapped the console and considered his options. His people rolled over immediately but it would take the pirates a while to get what they wanted. They might kill everyone at that point as they escaped...

If I can get a message to Alliance high command, I can get us some help. Ander tapped away at the console, bringing up the distress call. He needed to tight beam it or the pirates might pick up the signal. Filling the message with what he'd seen so far, he sent it out in three directions. It would have to reach someone...hopefully soon.

Now...to get to a safe place and gather some intel. Whoever gets here is going to need it. Ander didn't want his boredom to be cured by such a dramatic event but he had to admit, his adrenaline certainly was pumping. Had he not been in Subsection Six, he might not have been able to help.

Let's make this opportunity count, Ander...one way or another.

Chapter 1

"Anthar Mei'Gora!" His aide, Navan, called his name as he saluted and bowed his head. The old custom didn't set well with Mei'Gora but some of the more traditional families insisted on it. He returned the salute and waited for the young man's report. "I bring news from the new Earth ship. We have all but completed construction."

"Excellent news," Mei'Gora replied. "How much time before the ship is fully finished?"

"I'm afraid we've run into something of a problem, sir." Navan shifted on his feet. "We're out of Ulem, sir…the mineral to fire up the pulse engines. Our supply is totally exhausted."

"I seem to recall putting in a request for more recently." Mei'Gora checked his tablet. "Yes, I signed off on a consignment. Plenty to get the Earth what they needed for two more ships. What happened?"

"Um…well…that's part of the problem. Our primary mining facility, the one closest to Sol has come under attack."

Mei'Gora's eyes widened. "Not the enemy…"

"No. Pirates. Human and alliance from what our insider states."

"Insider?"

Navan nodded. "Yes, it seems a security guard was in a position to send us a distress call. He promises additional intel as he gathers it. For now, he stated the station was attacked and forced to surrender. Unfortunately, the news gets worse."

Mei'Gora rubbed his temples, eyes closed. "Do tell. How can it possibly get worse?"

"Somehow, these criminal scum have commandeered one of our own battle cruisers. Possibly the Aguna Spear which went missing in action last month."

"You're telling me these pirates have not only taken our mining facility but they also possess one of our combat vessels?"

"Yes, sir..." Navan looked nervous. "They seem to be interested in stealing our ore which will in turn elevate the current trade prices."

"I'm aware of the repercussions." Mei'Gora paced. "I'll report this to the humans. They'll be...unhappy I'm sure but perhaps we can turn this to our advantage."

"How?"

"Don't worry about it." Mei'Gora saluted the man. "Go about your business but keep this report between us. I'll disseminate the information to anyone who needs it."

"Yes, sir!" Navan offered a crisp salute and left the room.

How do we have such terrible luck lately? Mei'Gora received a communication from Clea about the ships they lost at the research facility. He looked forward to interrogating the prisoner personally. However, despite the fact that the team saved most of the research data, they lost an incredible amount in the exchange. So many ships...so many lives...

Pirates raiding their mining facilities felt like just one more stab from the fates, as if they didn't face enough challenges without the little extra. The human military council would not be pleased however, they may well be interested in a deal. Mei'Gora might have to bargain away a great deal for what he wanted but in the end, it would be worth it.

He sent a request for an emergency meeting and leaned back in his chair. At least they finished the structure of the new ship and began work on another. This potential fleet might end up turning the tide of the war but it would be useless without the final pieces to give them their high tech edge. Ulem provided a renewable energy unlike any other in the galaxy.

Pirates always tried to seize it. They never went for the source but with a cruiser under their command, such a bold move became possible...and successful. No station defense could withstand a battleship but then again, they'd gain nothing by destroying it. The station commander must've not be willing to call their bluff.

I wasn't there. The threat may have seemed credible.

Mei'Gora's request for a meeting with the human military council came back approved. They expected him in just over an hour so he changed into a dress uniform and had Navan arrange a shuttle. By the time he reached the hangar, launch preparations were complete so he boarded, taking a seat by the window near the front.

As the small ship departed his vessel, he peered out through the vastness of space at the large and now complete craft the humans built. With a little help from his own people and quite a few resources, they managed to get the thing to the very end of the development cycle. Just one more element was necessary to complete the project.

Mei'Gora took a deep breath and closed his eyes, mentally preparing himself to deliver the bad news. At least his offer would intrigue them. They may not take it or try to bargain for additional benefits but at least it would give them pause. Considering what they were promised for their trip to the research facility, he knew they'd be angry.

And rightly so. Time to turn a bad situation around…if that's even possible.

***

Daniel Burke had a bad feeling about the emergency meeting. The Kielans rarely did anything without notice and when they did, it tended to be reactionary to a problem. Whatever this request was about, it didn't bode well. Either the project was in jeopardy, they heard something about the Behemoth or another attack loomed ahead.

All three of those options gave Daniel heart burn.

Still, whatever the case might be, he forced himself to relax. They'd done pretty well so far with their defenses. The Kielan ship remained in orbit and the Tam'Dral was now crewed by a skilled military force. The refugees were on their way back to Alliance space where they would be provided a place to live while they plied their particular trades or received new training.

Maybe this problem will result in an opportunity for us. God, I hate the politics of it all.

Daniel spent the majority of his life as a leader of men, a soldier working through military tactics and strategy. With every promotion, his distance from the weeds increased until he found himself so far detached from day to day actions, he wouldn't know what specifically was going on if someone put a gun to his head.

Even fleet actions were below him now. He dealt with politicians and diplomats, men and women with more power than attention. They didn't want the details either but they required stories to tell their own people, positive ones to keep people happy or spins on the negative ones to bolster hope.

It started weighing on him not too long ago. Three years into his post, he struggled with what people expected of him and struggled against the types of requirements he worked under. Eventually, he came to terms with them because he saw the people waiting to take his role. They may not perform the job with the same amount of integrity so he clung to the position for the foreseeable future.

Daniel envied Gray Atwell. The captain of the Behemoth performed the exact job Daniel always wanted. Pioneering an experimental ship, defending the earth, leading people into battle...it quite possibly might be the most glorious post in the modern military. Sure, Gray didn't get to decide his missions but once he was out there, every decision was his and they all mattered.

Yesterday, I had to approve the new banners for the mess hall and sign off on a massive order cleaning supplies. Yes, this is definitely glamorous.

Alliance presence turned out to be good though. Having a whole ship of kielans available to assist with their building project helped but the cultural exchange mattered the most. As Earth looked to join the Alliance, they needed ambassadors from the military and engineering classes, people who would speak well of their new colleagues to the common folk.

So far, the plan seemed to be working. Much of the distrust he witnessed during the initial battle when Clea was assigned to them seemed to lessen. Collaboration became easier. Daniel truly believed integration would work out and as a result, Earth would take its place amongst its new allies without internal conflict putting a damper on the process.

Unless of course Mei'Gora has some kind of news which would ruin that hope.

Daniel entered the council chamber and took his seat, waiting as the others took positions around him. They held their own opinions, some negative and others self serving. For the most part, they worked toward preserving human interests in the galaxy but they definitely could learn to be more compromising.

"What does this kielan need?" Jameson asked. "We're very busy."

"We'll know soon enough," Daniel replied. "Honestly, Jameson, I would've hoped that you'd lighten up toward our allies by now. They did come to our aid when we needed it the most. Why do you consistently maintain a prejudiced sense toward them? It's ridiculous."

"Oh, is it?" Jameson glared. "They could've stayed instead of leaving us a single person. I don't feel they helped nearly as much as we needed."

"They saved the day," Daniel said. "What more did you want? They didn't even have to do that. You and I both know there were plenty of problems out there that they could've been dealing with rather than ours. Why would you think it's okay to give them grief over being kind? And believe me, they helped out of kindness."

"Don't be naive," Jameson waved his hand at Daniel. "You know they wanted more bodies for the war grinder. They needed us and as a result, we were saved."

"That makes no sense. Why would they help us on the hope we might have it in us to be of help? A better use of their resources would've been to stay out of it and clean up the mess...take what they want from our ashes. Instead, they let us preserve our way of life. I can't believe you'd look at that as some sort of ulterior motive."

"That's because I see with my eyes open and you're blinded by...whatever this is. Idealism...idiotic optimism."

"Okay, that's enough." Daniel started to get angry. "I can handle a debate but insubordination won't be tolerated."

"Sorry, sir." Jameson seemed to realize he'd crossed the line. "This is just a passionate subject for me."

"See that you govern that passion with some common sense." Daniel paused as the doors opened and guards stepped in and to the sides. Mei'Gora and his aide entered, moving for the podium at the center of the room. "Good afternoon, Anthar. How can we help you?"

"First, thank you for seeing me on such short notice," Mei'Gora said. "I'll get right to the point of my visit. Our project to finish your newest vessel is in jeopardy thanks to some vile criminals who have waylaid our nearest mining facility to the Earth."

"What does that mean for us?" Jameson asked.

"It's where I ordered the Ulem needed to ignite your new pulse drive," Mei'Gora replied. "I'm afraid these...these pirates have taken the station. Nothing will be leaving there until we reclaim it."

"And I suppose that means you need to leave, does it?" Jameson continued his attack. "As I suspected."

Mei'Gora shook his head. "No, it does not. I have a proposition for you, one which I hope will be of benefit to all involved."

"Explain." Daniel clasped his hands on the table.

"We received word that the Behemoth will be back soon. When it arrives, I recommend you send them to quell the criminals and take back the station." Mei'Gora lifted his hand to stave off questions before he finished. "In return, we will make all Ulem shipments to Earth a priority, allowing you to construct the rest of your fleet without being hampered by a lack of materials."

"What's the catch?" Marquel asked.

"I'm afraid the pirates have seized one of our warships," Mei'Gora said. "And so you'll have to contend with it when you get there. We'd rather you take it intact as well so we can put it back in the roster."

"Is that all?" Jameson shook his head. "You want our one ship to travel to your station, battle one of your ships without destroying it and what...take prisoners? Who are these pirates anyway?"

"Intelligence suggests they are comprised of both kielans and humans," Mei'Gora replied. "Meaning you have a stake in bringing them to justice as well. They've tried stealing shipments before but now, with the warship at their disposal, they're able to take the whole facility. I trust you'll appreciate the delicacy of the situation...and how my offer benefits your cause."

"And we would have priority requests for the shipments?" Daniel asked. "What about payment?"

"We were going to deliver the Ulem to you for free anyway to assist with the construction of your fleet," Mei'Gora said. "The better you are outfitted for war, the more you can help us win this conflict. Believe me, this isn't about profit. It's about bolstering our allies so we might survive, as a unified group against overwhelming odds."

"What intelligence can you offer on your station?" Elizabeth asked. "We'll need anything and everything at your disposal if we hope to be of use."

Mei'Gora nodded. "Of course. We will also stay on to help you with your third vessel. We truly want you to feel as if we're partnering with you in all ways. My ship could take care of this problem but our time is better spent assisting you with your shipbuilding projects."

Daniel stayed his people's comments with a raised hand. He looked down at his desk for several long moments before making a decision. "Okay, Anthar. What we would like from you is all the intel you can provide. Send it to us ASAP and we'll discuss amongst ourselves what we're going to do. As the Behemoth is not back yet, we seem to have some time to think, right?"

Mei'Gora bowed his head. "As you say."

"Thank you." Daniel stood up. "Once we have the information, we'll reconvene in my office, ladies and gentlemen. Thank you for your time. Good afternoon."

The team broke up and went their separate ways but before Daniel even sat down in his office, he had a message from Mei'Gora. The file contained floor plans and personnel records for everyone on board the mining facility. Flight schedules and work orders were also included and they were thorough enough to include previously employed individuals as well.

Daniel called the council back together right away and they began to deliberate. As he anticipated, Jameson was against the whole operation. Elizabeth took the middle ground. Others fought both ways. Some swayed between both sides of help or not to help. Ultimately, the discussion promised to go on for some time.

After six hours of conversation and pouring over the data exhaustively, they finally came to a consensus. They would send the Behemoth to the station and secure it against the pirates. Even the stodgiest opponents agreed the priority rights to Ulem outweighed the risks. The value of this assignment even outweighed the research facility fiasco.

At least this time we know they're going into a fight. That last one... Daniel shook his head. He contacted Mei'Gora himself to let him know their decision.

"Yes, Chief Burke?" Mei'Gora said. "I'm glad to hear from you...or at least, I hope I will be."

"You will," Daniel replied. "We've decided to take you up on your offer. When the Behemoth returns, we'll rearm her, resupply and send her to this mining facility."

"Excellent news, sir. Thank you."

"I must admit something, which I hope we can keep off the record."

Mei'Gora paused but replied, "certainly. What is it?"

"I have a concern. First, you research facility was compromised by the enemy. A traitor can't be controlled and it seemed one off. But now, we're talking about one of your big mining operations falling under the sway of pirates. I'm not feeling overly confident in your ability to defend yourselves."

"Believe me," Mei'Gora said, "we are fighting many battles. Our forces are stretched thin. I'm sure you know what that's like and what it means. We're not weak...but rather, overburdened. Your own history suggests you have cultures which know what that's like."

Daniel nodded. "Yes, true...I just hope that you'll be able to keep your end of the bargain when we have our fleet. We want to be partners, after all."

"Instead of saviors?" Mei'Gora asked. "I understand. Please remember what side of that we were on when we first met. But I don't think any of this matters. We're in a situation now. It is what it is and we can make it work together. We simply need to maintain mutual trust. If you can do so a little longer, I believe your patience will pay off."

"Agreed." Daniel leaned back in his chair. "Thank you for this candid conversation, Anthar. I appreciate it and I'll be sure to do you the same courtesy should the need ever arise."

"I'll take you up on the offer then, Chief Burke. Good day."

As the line went dead, Daniel studied his tablet. He needed to determine how he'd break the news to Gray, how to tell him they would be performing missions back to back. I'm sure they're up to the task, he thought, but then again, he had no idea how trying the research facility situation turned out to be.

Depending on what they reported, he might have to find some replacement people, some fresh troops to help them along. He looked into the roster to see who might be available but got distracted by messages demanding his attention. So many recruits joined the military once the Behemoth was almost done and they kept signing up every day.

Which is good, considering we've got two more ships on the way which will need crews. He'd been trying to think of who to appoint as captain of the next vessels and he'd shortened the list down to ten candidates. They would all be required to undergo a rigorous bout of questions from the council, though perhaps not as rough as what Gray experienced.

When they decided to put him in charge of the Behemoth, he had an advantage at being involved in the first battle but they really needed to know if he was up to the task of being the flagship commander. His bureaucratic skills were certainly up to snuff and his tactics could not be ignored. One of the papers he'd written in the academy remained a required study material for people entering command track.

Plus Daniel simply liked Gray. He was an easy man to work with and he knew when to push back and when to go with the flow. He could see the big picture without too much coaxing and tended to err on the side of conservative strategies. It made him ideal for working with the volatile council and more importantly, it made it him trustworthy with a priceless weapon of war.

Daniel remembered back to his Naval officer days and being at war. They fought one battle for three days straight before it came to a standstill. Men could handle fatigue, especially soldiers but the shelling back then rattled more than a few of them. The Behemoth crew might well be the most well trained military force in history.

He'd supervised much of it himself and saw it through in the updated academy programs. As often as he could, Daniel found his way down to the classrooms, to interact with the young minds who would one day take his place and defend their people against outside threats. They inspired him and kept him young, something he genuinely appreciated.

He believed in the new breed of soldier and knew that they had what it took to work under heavy stress for days on end. Their endurance was constantly put to the test through exams and physical training. They were the best and brightest in mind and body, working hard to get through tough courses and even tougher role play scenarios.

The Behemoth crew provided them with something to aspire to. Many of them had graduated with flying colors and experienced the change from the old way of studying to the new. Right in the middle of many of their terms, the courses had to change to reflect the new technology and they thrived.

Newer recruits didn't have to worry about such things. They dove right in without having to change gears in the middle of learning. As a result, they would come away with a brand new way of thinking, an entirely new breed of soldier and officer. Daniel lamented the loss of experience from the old way but he had to admit, it made sense.

This education gave the Behemoth crew a distinct advantage going into multiple conflicts and situations. Daniel believed in them wholeheartedly and still envied them, even if they didn't get any rest before heading back out into space. At least they won't be expected to approve the tableware for the banquet hall...or a request for the military band to go on a global tour.

Yeah, Gray...I think you might have it better than me. I hope you agree. I'm afraid you won't have any choice either way.

Chapter 2

The Behemoth didn't attempt another jump immediately but they did maneuver well away from their entry point and positioned themselves near a small planetoid, inhospitable to human life. There, they performed some routine maintenance and really looked at the engines. A full day of repairs and analytics later, they got underway under normal engines.

They'd jump when they had a chance to lick their wounds and get the ship in better condition. Gray didn't like the idea of throwing themselves into something unnecessary but he kept them on the verge of hyperspace at a moment's notice, in case the enemy had a way of tracking them.

When no one showed up in the system, everyone relaxed as much as they could. Being in a strange sector didn't do much for nerves but with no one shooting at them, they couldn't complain too much. After some decent down time and normal duties, even two days did wonders. Doctor Brand even gave her blessing for a swifter trip home.

Gray finally gave the order at the first shift of the third day. They prepped and jumped back into Sol space near Neptune. Their trip back to Earth would take some time, additional relaxation for the crew. Once they arrived, they received a message which made the captain glad for his decision: a priority request from Daniel Burke.

Gray took the communication in his office, bringing the older man up on the screen.

"Gray," Daniel greeted him with a smile, "welcome back! You look no worse the wear. Got a report for me?"

"How much do you already know, sir?"

"Quite a lot actually. The Alliance told us most of the situation...that you guys were ambushed when you arrived in the sector and had to fight your way through getting the research. Saved a lot of lives from what I hear."

"Yeah, I've got some stowaways aboard," Gray replied. "They'll probably want to rejoin the Alliance ship as soon as we get there. As for us, our damage is minor. We've repaired most of it after holing up in an adjacent sector. Once the ship was jump worthy, we came home. I estimate we'll be back to Earth in a couple days."

"How'd she operate? Everything work as expected?"

"Yes, she's held her own. We've found some issues with the jump drive that we're working out and learned some new tactics from our allies, which will require some extra work to our equipment but all around, I'd say we've got an incredible ship. If the other two are half as well put together, we'll be in good shape."

"I'm glad to hear it. I've been worried about how she'd hold up in combat, how she would fare under real stress tests."

"Believe me, we've put this ship through the paces. She's not brand new anymore and as she settles in, we're definitely learning how to get the most out of her." Gray hesitated. "Have you decided who will command the new ships?"

"I've been thinking about it and have a short list of candidates. Why, do you have a suggestion?"

Gray hesitated for only a moment. "Commander Everly would make a good choice. You should at least talk to him. He's got the advantage of knowing how these operate and what to expect. Plus, he's seen the enemy up close and personal. That should give him an edge over those who haven't fought yet."

"Good point. I hadn't considered Adam but I really should have. Has he nipped some of his impulsiveness in the bud?"

"I'm still coaching him out of that but I'm confident he'll come around." Gray smirked. "I seem to remember you had a bit of that when you were a newer captain."

"Yes, but the stakes weren't as high then. Now, we need pretty much perfect men to do the job right. You know what I'm talking about too. We can't afford crazy risks. Losing one of those ships would be catastrophic."

"Understood. Well…" Gray shrugged. "At least think about it."

"I'll certainly have a conversation with him. He deserves that much." Daniel paused a moment. "I hate to change the subject, but I've got a new assignment for you when you get here, another trip beyond our borders."

Gray's stomach sank. Another engagement with the enemy did not pique his interest. Frankly, he'd hoped for a little time off for himself. Battling the alien invaders took a lot out of a man and though he knew he could handle more, he didn't enjoy the idea of having to. Especially considering what they'd all seen.

"What's going on, Daniel?"

"Pirates, surprisingly." Daniel sighed. "They took over a mining facility belonging to the alliance and get this, they somehow stole one of their battleships."

Much as the situation sounded dire, Gray couldn't help but feel relieved. Tension in his shoulders loosened and he sank into his chair. Rubbing his eyes, he focused on what he just heard and found himself in a state of disbelief. What kind of brazen criminals could possibly do what he just described?

"That's incredible. How? I've seen those things in action and under competent command, they can hold their own against the enemy pretty well." Gray felt a tinge of worry for Kale. He still hoped the man somehow survived.

"Then we're even more worried about it," Daniel replied. "We don't know how the pirates seized the vessel but they sure did. Apparently, they try to steal shipments all the time but they finally had the means to take the whole damn facility and exercised it. Now, they've got a lot of hostages."

"So what do you want us to do?"

"We need you to reclaim the facility. There are a lot of innocent people on board, basically hostages now. They, and the structure, need to be taken intact."

"Do we know how many people we're talking about?"

"It's in the intel," Daniel said. "The other objective is to take back the battleship. We need that with minimal damage as well."

"Wait, I have to somehow disable the ship?" Gray considered the objective for a moment. "It might not even be possible. Depending on the command these people have of the systems on there, it could be incredibly dangerous, especially with limiting rules of engagement. I'll definitely try but I'd be crazy to give a guarantee."

"Understood. Your primary duty is to defend the Behemoth but if it looks like you can't possibly save the battleship, then do what you have to do. In fact, I'd rather you destroy it than leave it in pirate hands. But consider this: if we pull this off, it'll be a big win. We'll get priority shipping privileges with the mine and they'll stay on to help us with the third ship."

"How close is the second one to being complete?"

"Oh, it was close enough to being done that a little Alliance tech pushed it over the edge." Daniel hesitated for a moment. Gray began to think the line dropped when the Chief spoke again. "The trouble involved the element to ignite the engines. That's how they learned their station had been compromised."

Gray sighed. "Should I just turn around now? I'm sure we could get to the mine pretty fast and get on it."

"No, bring in the Alliance personnel. You can't have them on board while you're out there. Plus, I'd feel better if you rearmed and resupplied. Yes, we're in a hurry but not at the expense of mission success. You can deploy shortly after. Will that work?"

"Yes, I'll meet with my department heads about it. Can you get me the intel?"

"It's already on the way and you should have it in your mailbox. Go over it and let us know if you need anything else when you get here. I trust your judgement about this but we're here to help so don't hesitate to use us. We've got some good ideas...well, we do once in a while."

"You've already seen this information," Gray said. "You really think we can take it all alone, huh?"

"It's a mining facility so sparsely armed. Even if they manned those cannons they can't get through your shields and the Behemoth is a mobile military base. You've got everything you need to occupy a small country. I have total faith you can take it back and hold it if need be."

"That's good enough for me." Gray took a deep breath. "Thank you for your confidence, Sir. We'll talk soon."

Gray killed the communicator and brought up the message he received. The Alliance had been thorough with their documentation, far more than Gray anticipated. He read through it all before sending out a meeting request to his people. They'd have to discuss it before heading to meet the threat.

Especially the marines. This would be a heavy task for them as they had to not only clear the station but an entire starship as well. Providing they could figure out a way to get them on board the ship. He hoped Clea had an answer. On the surface, it didn't look possible to take the craft intact but he'd long since given up saying something couldn't happen.

He sent his people the intel and went to the briefing room to wait. In a half hour, they'd plan their next engagement. At least this time it didn't involve the true enemy. He'd grown tired of dealing with their suicidal zeal. He wanted a straight forward situation, something where the opponent cared enough about their own lives to behave rationally.

Considering all he saw during their last fight, the fact that the enemy threw away entire star cruisers and sacrificed their own lives several times to gain an advantage, he wanted a foe with some humanity. It seemed odd to think it, especially since it shouldn't be better. He could relate to pirates on some level. They were more like him.

The enemy, on the other hand, didn't think like them at all. They were alien in every sense of the word. That alone made them something to be afraid of. He chose not to be, fought against fear because deep down, he knew they were simply unknown—not supernatural or even more than a bunch of religious zealots.

Humanity faced threats like them many times in history and those were from other, rational humans. Religious infighting caused no end of trouble for the nations of Earth for as far back as history was recorded. It helped to keep that in mind while they faced the enemy but it didn't make it easier when they lost people as a result of their horror.

Pirates may be many things but they rarely proved willing to die for a cause. Gray was counting on that. They wanted a quick buck, not to make a statement. All he had to do was get some of his people aboard and some superior firepower would take care of the rest. I love how simple it sounds in my head. If only I were young enough to believe my own bravado.

***

Rathe Darnell commanded the pirates, if one could truly lead such a rabble. Both human and kielan personnel worked his ship, which was how they managed to capture the battleship. However, the station took a different kind of experience and knowledge, something they didn't have before they took a freighter of supplies heading for the station.

Thantis…whatever his surname was…had been en route back to the station. He'd been let go after an accident scarred him terribly and left him with a limp. Working as a specialist in Alliance tech, he'd been responsible for the reactors keeping the place aloft. He knew every access tunnel and precisely where to shoot to do the least amount of damage but to make an impression.

Rathe didn't trust Thantis completely but the man definitely wanted to get back at the government for what happened to him. When they boarded the station, the lean man seemed particularly pleased to be back. He immediately set about assessing the security systems and suddenly started to laugh.

"They didn't make any significant changes or improvements," Thantis said. "My passwords still work.

These idiots! They shouldn't have gotten rid of me! Apparently, none of them understand the concept of protection or being careful. I'll have full access to the network in a moment...then we can have the cargo moved into position to take."

"Excellent." Rathe watched him for a moment, wondering if the guy might be a little unbalanced. It didn't really matter. Most of them were a little crazy for taking on the super powers during a war. But that's where the profits were. Tiny cuts in the rear while they were all focused outward. "We're going to secure people in their homes. Can you cut their access so they'll keep quiet?"

"Yes, of course. None of them have access to anything from those little holes so it'll be fine. Just seal the doors and they'll be like luxurious little cells." Thantis shook his head. "To think I ever liked being here. It's insulting."

"Sure..." Rathe shook his head and turned to one of the kielans on his crew. "Xurn, grab as many guys as you need and herd these cows to where they belong, okay?"

Xurn tilted his head. "Cows?"

Rathe rolled his eyes. "Um...cattle? Herd animals? Any of that ring in your kielan head?"

"Ah, yes...like the belicons."

"Sure...those...get them to their rooms." Rathe rubbed his temples. "Thantis, how long before you're done with everything? We've been here...well...we've been here too long."

It had taken forever to get boarded and secure the people in the promenade. His own forces swept the entire inhabited area. The security didn't put up a fight but finding every nook and cranny took the better part of a day. When they finally got them into one place to watch, Rathe finally took the control center.

Thantis began his magic but it didn't look like it would be quick.

"A few hours," Thantis said. "Maybe a little more. These computers are slow. Plus, we've got to move all the Ulem. That'll take the better part of a day."

"Excellent..." Rathe sat down. "So we're here for a while. I hope you're right about no one getting a message out. If the Alliance shows up..."

"What? You'll blow them out of the sky with their own ship." Thantis waved his hand at him. "Or take another and build a fleet. Even if they bring a dozen warships, it won't matter. We have hostages and they'll never risk civilians, believe me. We're going to be fine."

Rathe's experience with the military didn't put them in such a light. He thought they may well blow up the station before allowing pirates to make away with all the goods. Of course, the only way anyone would find out they held control over the station was when the shipments became late.

"Get me the shipping schedule," Rathe said. "And let me know when you're close to being done. I want this place under tight control as soon as possible."

***

Clea sat in her quarters staring at the ceiling when the call for a meeting came over her tablet. She checked, saw Gray was the organizer and sat up. She'd enjoyed her downtime but it came with a price. Her mind continually drifted to her family and specifically her sister. The woman's treachery made Clea sick, so much so she had no idea how to break the news to their parents.

They were kind hearted people, the type that wouldn't know how to respond to the news she had. Betrayal didn't make sense to them. Other traitors had been discovered and their efforts broadcast to the population. She remembered her parents finding it totally unfathomable that anyone would do such a thing.

Most of the people in her family were considered patriots. When they learned what Vora did, they would certainly disown her. The next step would be to distance themselves. The woman Clea grew up with would be stricken from the family history books, her images removed from albums and any mention of her would be frowned upon.

For all intents and purposes, Clea no longer had a sister. Maybe she shouldn't be sad about it. Maybe the sorrow she felt was misplaced but she was too kind hearted to be callous. Her father might well tell her she shouldn't waste her grief on Vora. Her mother, whether or not she agreed, would do so publicly.

She envisioned being alone with her feelings and if she didn't want to experience a lot of familial drama, she would need to remain silent. The last thing they needed was dissent in their ranks. Then again, the chances of her seeing her parents anytime soon were incredibly small. It wasn't like she had a plan to visit in the next few days.

Clea pulled on her jacket and looked at herself in the mirror. The woman looking back seemed exhausted though none of the typical signs marred her face. No dark circles, no slouch in posture. Her silver-blue eyes simply lacked their normal luster. Sorrow mixed with exhaustion. Everything that happened back at the research facility left her feeling empty.

Gathering the data and saving the people worked out but all the Alliance ships and crew…poor decisions, poor thinking cost them all. Then Kale seemingly sacrificed himself. She didn't want to believe it. Not in her heart. He'd proven to be a solid commander and to have lost him was a great blow to their cause.

And seven more ships. Don't forget that number.

Their armada could withstand quite a lot and manufacturing plants on their home world produced ships fairly quickly. That's why the human ship wouldn't take long for them. Mei'Gora surely brought a fabrication unit to assist with the longer parts oft he job. Clea petitioned for one several times but her commanders refused.

They didn't trust humanity with such technology back then. Now, they might not have a choice.

Gray proved to be a cunning commander, the type the Alliance needed. Many of the kielan Anthars relied on traditional tactics and they partially worked. They didn't always result in victory though and men like

Kale switched it up. Creative thinkers began to take over the fighting and, in Clea's opinion, that's precisely what they needed.

Clea settled her hair, grabbed her tablet and headed for the meeting. An email explained the situation and included a file about pirates. They captured an Alliance mining facility. Wow, just when I thought we couldn't possibly get more bad news. Hostages were involved and the kicker came from the commandeered Alliance warship.

They stole a warship? How? That Anthar's out of a job...if he's still alive.

She flipped through the layout of the station and finished just as she stepped into the briefing room. Gray was there alone and she sat to his left. "Hello," she said without looking up from her studies. "This is awful."

"But hopefully easier than the last two things we did," Gray said. "How're you feeling? You seem..."

"Tired?" Clea offered.

Gray shrugged.

"Sad?"

"Maybe a little of both." Gray tilted his head. "Everything catching up to you?"

"I wouldn't say that...I just...I guess I've had too much time to think."

"That's the enemy of every soldier ever," Gray replied. "But your conscience should be clear. You've acted with integrity in everything you've done as far as I'm concerned."

"The military part of our actions don't bother me," Clea said. "The family part, the personal aspects...those are what weigh on my heart. I'll figure it out. It will not effect my performance. I promise."

"I never imagined it would." Gray patted her arm. "Believe me, I'm more worried about my performance than yours."

Clea's brow wrinkled. "Do you have doubts, Captain?"

"Doubts? No...concerns? Worries? Things that upset me? Losing men, Kale...those bother me. I don't second guess but I do spend time trying to figure out what I could've done better to avoid losses.

Retrospective analysis is not a bad thing as long as you don't become mired in second guesses. Those are pretty much the bane of any commander."

The department heads began filing in and shortly after they began the briefing. Gray went over their intelligence thoroughly and explained the situation about the battleship, the hostages and what humanity hoped to gain by getting involved. They needed to be quick in getting out there before the pirates got away or hurt anyone.

Chief Engineer Maury Higgins reported critical repairs were complete and they were wrapping up a few smaller projects, all of which would be done before they jumped again. They went over the drive several times but would need to consult with one of the Alliance experts before they performed another microjump.

"I just can't trust that it'll make it through another one, Captain. Not after what we experienced before."

Gray nodded. "Understood. I'm not sure we'll have to this time but we can jump, right?"

"Yes, standard jumps with plenty of plot time are no problem," Maury said. "The engines get a steady and measured flow of energy that way."

"Perfect." Gray turned to Lieutenant Colonel Marshall Dupont. "The majority of this op falls on your marines."

"We have plenty of men ready for such an exercise," Marshall replied. "Those men who went on the ground op don't have to be involved though Hoffner will likely insist. It sounds like we're going to need two contingents, providing you can get us on the other ship."

"That's definitely on us," Gray said. "Anyone else have any concerns about this before we go?"

Group Commander Estaban Revente spoke up, "the briefing suggests that the pirates make heavy use of drones. I looked at the schematics and they don't seem too bad. Fairly maneuverable but still reliant on someone to control them. However, what concerns me are their pilots."

Gray nodded. "Explain."

"Reports suggest these pirates have little regard for their own safety," Estaban said. "This makes them unpredictable and frankly, more dangerous. Are they going to pull some insane maneuver that puts them in as much jeopardy as the ship they're battling? We won't know until we're out there."

"Can your pilots handle them?" Adam asked.

Estaban smirked. "Of course...but we can't ignore the threat. Suicidal pilots in space are a concern."

"Noted." Gray turned to the rest of the team. "Anyone else?"

"How're we going to get on the ship without damaging it?" Lieutenant Commander Stephanie Redding asked. She was the pilot. "If they have their shields up, a shuttle isn't going to hop through."

"I believe I may have a solution," Clea replied. "When we get back to Earth, I'll update my tablet's database with the latest information from the Alliance ship registry. Our computer systems have backdoors which I may be able to utilize in order to shut it down and give you the opportunity to land."

"There wasn't much certainty in what you said," Marshall said. "How're you not sure?"

"Because if they were clever enough to take one of our ships, they might've been smart enough to mess with the computers." Clea shrugged. "I'll work with Lieutenant Darnell and familiarize him with our programming languages. Together, we should be able to get something done."

"The station looks pretty big," Commander Adam Everly said, leaning over the tactical map. "And those pirates could be anywhere. It looks like a nightmare to me."

"Not as bad as you think," Maury answered. "They've got a huge contingency of hostages to watch. Even if they locked them up, they need to keep them under guard. Plus their men are divided between the ship and the station. A battleship can't be managed by a skeleton crew, not effectively."

Gray added, "and if it is, then we'll have a distinct advantage."

"We also have the insider," Clea added. "If you didn't notice, we received the update from a security guard who was away from the main part of the station when the attack happened. He's held up somewhere in the maintenance corridors and promised to provide additional intel as he can."

"Do we know who he is?" Marshall asked.

"He identified himself as Ander Yin'Dran. I checked against our database. He's a former soldier with a solid record." Clea looked up from her tablet. "I'd trust whatever he has to say about the situation. Chances are good he'll have solid tactical data to share, the kind which might save some lives."

"We should link up with him on board then," Marshall replied. "If he knows the layout, he can help us get around, find advantages on the targets so we can take them out easier. Sounds like an ace in the hole for us."

"Good," Gray said. "We'll try to find a covert way to make contact upon arrival. Any other thoughts?"

"Let's go over all the exit points again," Marshall said. "When I take this to the marines, I want to give them a solid idea of where everything is. Maintenance, reactor, living quarters, control center, everything."

Clea participated in the briefing but mostly allowed them to work through their boarding plans. Her mind was occupied on how they might take back the Alliance ship. Considering the complexity of the vessel, she had no idea how anyone but a trained professional might be flying it, let alone keeping it in maintenance.

She prepared a set of instructions for Oliver Darnell, something to give him a firm understanding of what to expect. When they sat down together to hack into the ship, they would need to be able to think on the fly, to work together rapidly or they would tip themselves off. Any mistake might lead to an open conflict, one they could not necessarily afford.

Chapter 3

The Behemoth returned home and immediately went about resupplying and rearming. Clea visited Mei'Gora to procure the updated database. She also received her promotion to Su-Anthar as promised. The honor was bittersweet as she turned over the prisoner and all the people they saved from the planet and damaged ships.

Later, she and Darnell worked through the programming protocols but he proved to already know what she planned to teach. "During the construction of the Behemoth, I worked with you then and later, I studied your Universal Code, remember?"

"You're a remarkable young officer." Clea clapped him on the shoulder. "Start thinking about how we're going to get through their defenses. Their shields will block any attempt to remotely connect to their computers so I believe we need to get them to drop them."

"Maybe." Olly shrugged. "I'm reading the technical specs on Alliance ship defenses now. There might be a way around that."

"If you find one, let me know...we'll have to close the loop."

Olly grinned. "Absolutely, ma'am."

Many of the crew took advantage of the several hours off to get some rest or even drop down to Earth to visit friends and loved ones. They had a sixteen hour gap between arrival and departure. Those who had to work did so feverishly with the promise of being able to get some sleep on the way out to a safe trajectory for a jump.

At the designated time, Clea came to the bridge, joining Gray at the same time. They both took their seats and he turned to Adam, offering him a nod. The first officer stood and clasped his hands behind his back.

"Okay, Redding. Take us out."

"Aye, sir." Redding engaged the thrusters and pulled away from Earth orbit.

"Lieutenant Collins," Adam turned to the navigator, Timothy. "Set a course for the open space between the moon and Mars. Then plot us a jump. I believe you have the numbers for that?"

"Yes, sir. I've been programming them in all morning." Tim worked his console for a moment before turning to Redding. "It's all yours. Just follow the pretty blue line."

"I love it when you make it blue." Redding grinned. "It's green way too often."

"I like green," Tim replied. "Olly, can you please double check my jump coordinates to ensure they're optimal?"

"Already done," Olly said. "They look good. No adjustments recommended."

"Thank you."

Redding glanced back at Adam. "Sir, we're ready to initiate full thrust. ETA to jump point, thirty-five minutes."

Adam nodded. "Go ahead."

Clea's mind drifted as the ship got underway. She thought back to the moment she turned Vora An'Tufal, her sister, over to Mei'Gora as a traitor. Two human soldiers acted as guards and walked behind them with their guns at the ready. Vora changed from the moment she got on board the Behemoth to when Clea came to fetch her prisoner transfer.

"It's time," Clea announced but her sister did not look up. She merely stood and offered her hands so they could be bound. "Anthar Mei'Gora is here. He'll be arranging transport back home where you'll stand trial."

"After a lengthy interrogation no doubt," Vora replied.

Clea nodded. "Undoubtedly."

As they walked down the hall together, Clea tried to think of something to say, something which might bring closure to the situation but nothing came to mind. Ultimately, she chose to remain silent as they boarded a shuttle and flew for the Alliance ship. Clea knew that once Vora left her custody, her sister would be gone forever. They'd very likely execute her for treason.

Bitterness filled her heart but it battled sadness. Why had her own blood betrayed them? The answers weren't satisfactory and probably never would be. Moments before they docked, she turned to her sibling and grabbed her arm tightly, scowling at her. It drew the other woman's attention who scowled but did not reply.

"I loved you," Clea said. "Even though you treated me so poorly so often, I still loved you. Right now, on the verge of turning you over to the military for trial, I continue to feel…for you. It won't go away, no matter how I try to smother it or make it vanish."

Vora's expression lightened for the first time since Clea found her on the research facility. A sad smile touched her lips. "Listen to me, Clea…forget me. That's your best bet and my best offer. If you do not, if you cling to some past we shared, what happens next will only be harder. I'll accept my fate for what I've done. You don't have to go through it with me."

"Family is supposed to stick together."

"And I abandoned you all," Vora spoke sternly. "Regardless of belief or ideology, right or wrong, I stood for myself. Not my people, not mother and father...not you. I was selfish and now I'll pay for it. But please...you have to let me go."

"I don't know if I can."

"Eventually, then. You'll figure it out." Vora turned and looked out the view port. "You won't have a choice, little sister."

They didn't speak again, not even when Mei'Gora met them in the hangar with four armed guards who roughly escorted Vora away. The Anthar watched them go then turned his attention to Clea, giving her a cool assessment as his eyes raked over her. For a brief moment, she privately hated him. How could he remain so cool under the circumstances?

It's not his family member...

"Excellent work, Vinthari An'Tufal. Thank you for bringing this prisoner to us personally."

"It seemed appropriate," Clea replied. "Given the circumstances."

"Of course." Mei'Gora patted her shoulder. "I'm sure this must be difficult for you but believe me that this was the right thing to do. Vora An'Tufal betrayed us all and nearly ruined everything."

"I know…"

"We'll have a ceremony later." Mei'Gora reached into his pocket and revealed a small box. "But for now, it's official. You are Su-Anthar An'Tufal. Congratulations." He removed her old rank from her collar and replaced it with the new one. She took the extras for her other uniform from him with numb fingers.

"Thank you, sir." A promotion right on the heels of turning in her sister felt…wrong. Still, she did what she had to do. Accepting it with grace and humility kept her from crying. Focusing on duty and tradition helped her get over the hurdle of her sister's betrayal. "I appreciate the gesture."

"You earned it. I believe you have a new assignment."

"Our mining facility…and a ship." Clea's brows furrowed. "Why are you sending the Earth ship instead of our own? I would've imagined we'd rather take care of our own mess."

"Another test," Mei'Gora said. "One I believe they'll pass with flying colors."

"I can tell you, they should no longer be tested, sir. They have proven to be creative thinkers...we're the only ship to have escaped the research facility alive."

"I'm aware of that," Mei'Gora replied. "But any feather in the cap of humanity is one they can cash in for their seat on our council...and I can tell you they want it badly. Some of them are resistant, still living in some strange past where isolationism is an option but they'll come around. All of them will...and it'll be easier when they have all the currency in the world to trade for a say in galactic politics."

"I at least have faith that many of them are up to the responsibility," Clea said. "The people I work with are not like those...those isolationists. They work for everyone, risking their lives for people they never met, for another race entirely. I think when they have their say, we won't be sorry."

"We have our own naysayers, of course, but their voices are far quieter due to the fact that we've allowed so many to join us." Mei'Gora smiled. "The alliance may have found many setbacks but we're learning to get around them and eventually, we'll win this war. People like you and those you serve with are our ambassadors."

"As you say." Clea bowed her head. "Thank you again. I should return to the Behemoth."

"Help them anyway you can, Clea." Mei'Gora waved. "They'll need it."

As the ship prepared to jump, she shook her head at the reverie. Gray and the crew probably did not need her for much. Sure, she had some insights that they found useful but for the most part, they handled themselves just fine. Her contributions were minor, mostly having to do with alliance technology.

Clea didn't feel like the most qualified person for that job even. But then, her confidence was shaken by the events on the research facility. Not too badly, perhaps rattled was a better term. The violence itself didn't bother her but the needless waste…even the enemy sacrificing their own ships made her sick to her stomach.

How could they throw people away so casually? Destroy so many lives without a second thought? Just for a quick victory! Gray and Kale even used it against them, allowing them to destroy a vessel for no reason. She found herself pitying the enemy far more than hating them. The rank and file soldier must've been terribly brainwashed.

Olly broke her thoughts, "when we jump into their space, they're obviously going to know right away. Do you want me to start jamming right when we have control?"

"Yes," Gray replied. "Marines are already boarded into drop ships. You start the jamming and they'll launch, getting as far from the ship as they can without being detected. We'll open negotiations in an attempt to get them access to both the station and the starship. If all goes well, we should have both back in a few hours."

Adam shook his head. "How often do things go according to plan around here?"

"On the better side of never," Gray said. "But I like to be optimistic. Keeps me young."

"At least something does," Adam replied. "Because it sure isn't our luck."

"Oh, I don't know." Gray leaned back in his chair. "It hasn't been bad so far. We're still alive, aren't we? And look at all we've accomplished. I think we're fine and this mission is as straight forward as we're likely to get for a long time. Go ahead and initiate the jump, Redding. I'd like to have a chat with these pirates."

Clea considered Ander and wondered what exactly was going on for him. He'd been in a dangerous situation for well over a day already and no other messages left the station. Was he okay? Did he survive? Or had he been captured? Part of her wanted to believe he was still on the loose, harassing the pirates and keeping them from completing their objectives.

The rational side of her felt like he might not be alive. Such heroes rarely got away with guerrilla activities for long, especially in confined spaces. Yes, the station was big but ultimately, it was contained. Escape required a ship or escape pod and either of those would be quickly detected. No, if he was on board he likely had to lay low or be caught.

Either way, they'd know soon. If the pirates found out he sent the warning, they'd definitely be looking for him. And if they didn't, then he could indeed be the ace Marshall talked about at the briefing. One way or another, Ander might play a major part in their reclamation of the station.

Even if he was no longer alive.

***

Ander needed supplies. The nourishment in the lower levels was emergency only and when he found it, the ration packs had expired almost a year back. He had no idea how long he'd been down there before help came. Sending the message was only stage one in what he needed to accomplish.

Now, he needed to maintain his strength so he could gather information on the pirates for whoever arrived.

When the station surrendered to the pirates, the criminals still needed to board the place and lock it down. Minimal space safety required them to do it properly. Somewhere, they docked a larger craft, not the battleship but something else. It took hours for them to get it right and when they did, they had to board the place.

Security folded in minutes. Ander watched in horror on one of the vid screens as the pirates just came in and disarmed his peers. I could've been one of them. Once security was pacified, the civilian population didn't put up a fight. At first, they were held in the promenade but Ander figured they'd get moved eventually.

Next, the pirates conducted a sweep of the entire station, essentially looking for people like Ander. They found several, miners working early and maintenance crews who didn't hear the call to surrender.

Only a few of them put up resistance but they were rewarded with a beating that kept other people in line.

It took them the better part of a day and a half before they truly held the station. Ander wasn't surprised. His home supported countless families. That's what bothered him the most. Children were up there, subjected to these criminal scum there to steal. This wasn't political or ideologically motivated. It came down to money.

Sickening.

A pessimistic part of him worried that no one got his message. Fear gripped his heart that no reinforcements might arrive. If that turned out to be true, then he might be the only person who could stop the pirates from killing everyone. He believed wholeheartedly that no one on the station was meant to survive.

Even if the criminals got what they wanted, killing everyone aboard made more sense than letting them live. Witnesses might tell the Alliance about the ship or their numbers, their weapons...anything to get them caught when they surfaced with their stolen goods. Ander would not let that happen, regardless of what it took.

But first, he needed some water. Actual starvation or dehydration wouldn't kick in for a while but the first thing he learned in basic training with the military involved setting up a supply chain for any prolonged operations. He'd set up a fortified base in a shut down security check point deep inside Subsection Six, far away from anywhere people ever went.

Maintenance tunnels nearby allowed him access to the entire station at the expense of convenience. Anywhere he wanted to go involved climbing ladders which made getting to the highest levels impractical. He couldn't storm the bridge from down there, not without some kind of power assisted armor.

I wish I had some of that from the army still.

The promenade was only four floors up, nothing to joke about but close enough to be practical. He checked his weapon and ventured out. Access tunnels were behind sealed doors with manual releases.

Everything down there was practical and didn't always run on power. The idea was that if something happened to the reactor, crews could still operate and repair the place.

It worked to Ander's advantage but one thing he remembered was the doors could be incredibly loud. Trying to be quiet meant exerting more energy to absorb the noise. He grabbed the massive metal ring and began to turn, tensing up just as much as might be necessary to break the seal.

When he felt it give, he stopped then pressed again until the door came open. He peeked into the dark and his heart fell for a moment. Then he realized it would work to his advantage. No one would casually see him if they looked in but then again, he'd have to scale the ladder in the dark.

I guess there are worse things.

Ander grabbed the rungs and began to ascend, counting each step he took before reaching the landing. He anticipated no more than ten to fifteen rungs. When he got to thirty-five, he began to get nervous. At fifty, he finally reached the first landing and he flopped onto it, breathing heavily.

It wasn't that he was out of shape but the anxiety of climbing in the dark combined with more exertion than he anticipated worked at his nerves. His arms felt heavy despite the fact that he'd made many harder climbs in his day. The worst part was he had to do it three more times to get to his destination.

Ander allowed himself nearly twenty minutes of rest before he started climbing again. This time, he was ready for the workout but by the end, he was still winded and his body trembled. Lying on his back, he stretched his arms over his head and brought his knees to his chest, trying to loosen up the muscles.

Knots formed in his biceps but he worked them out over time until he felt mostly prepared to head out into the promenade for his much needed supplies.

Ander's heart fell again. I have to climb back down that thing.

Providing he survived.

Ander twisted the dial on the door, repeating his performance from down below. As the seal broke, he carefully turned it to avoid any loud noises. When it opened, he drew his weapon and peeked out. No one was around and he found himself in the loading area for the cafe where he got his drink before the attack.

Pacing out, he strained to hear, listening for any activity out in the promenade. Footsteps made him freeze and a couple voices chatting nearby.

"You done?" The first guy sounded like he shouted a lot, his throat hoarse and gravely. "I got my section cleared out."

"Yeah, I'm done." The other man was higher pitched, almost like one imagined a rodent. "They didn't give me any guff. Just went along quietly. I think they had to use the can."

"Damn station bound losers," Gravely said. He made a spitting noise. "Hate these cowards. It would be nice to have a real fight on our hands, you know? Someone who actually resisted. This just feels too easy. Like we're doing something legal."

"I'd rather not be shot at," Rodent replied. "Easy jobs just mean we get a quicker payout. And there's nothing wrong with that, you know?"

"I guess. Still. Killing someone would be nice." Gravely paused. "This place has juice...it says real fruit."

"No way..." Rodent gasped. "You're right! Oh, I'm getting some of that."

Damn it! Ander clenched his fist. He needed access to the diner and if these two goons were sitting around enjoying smoothies, he'd be stuck. The longer he stood around out there, the greater his chance of being caught. The only other place to get his supplies sat on the far end of the promenade, a small outlet for groceries.

It's this place or none...How do I get them out of there?

"Hey, who the hell are you?" The man's voice made Ander freeze and his blood pumped hot through his system. He glanced over his shoulder and saw a confused looking man wearing a tattered tee shirt and cargo pants tucked into scuffed boots. His weapon remained slung over his shoulder as he admired Ander. "You can't possibly be station security..."

"I am." Ander pointed his gun at the guy. "Keep quiet or I'll shoot."

"You...wait a minute, you really are with security! How? We rounded you lot up!"

"Not all of us I guess." Ander gestured to the wall. "Put your hands on that. Now!"

The bewildered pirate placed his hands on the wall, shaking his head. "This is amazing...I thought we'd cleared this place."

Ander checked him over and relieved the man of his rifle. Slinging it on his shoulder, he found the man's identification. Harvin Lank. The name meant nothing to Ander but he thrust it in his pocket.

"I don't know what you plan to do, copper but um...we hold the whole station. What do you think arresting me is going to do anyway?"

"Shut up!" Ander shoved him into the wall. "Keep your voice down!"

"Why?" Harvin glanced over his shoulder. "Are you worried about the others just around the corner? I know they're out there. I was coming to meet them."

"Last warning. Next time, I'll just fire."

"And give away your position? I doubt it."

"It won't matter to you, will it?"

"Help!" Harvin shouted.

Ander's shoulders slumped. Bastard! He slammed the butt of his pistol against Harvin's neck hard enough to make him crumple to the floor, unconscious. Ander looked around frantically, unsure what to do. If he simply left, his potential prisoner would give him away. The rest of the pirates would start looking for him.

On the alternative, killing these men would likely give him away too unless they simply...disappeared. A desperate idea struck him, one he didn't feel proud of but it would certainly work. It involved killing, something he hadn't done since the war but in this case, his survival and many people on the station depended on him maintaining his freedom.

Ander pressed his back against the wall and aimed his weapon toward where he heard the pirates. Their footsteps indicated he had moments before they'd be on him. Their shadows loomed against the wall. Gravely spoke up, "Harvin, is that you? What the hell are you doing back there? The bathroom's open, man."

Ander's hand trembled for just a moment before he mastered himself, falling into his soldier ways again. He tilted his head down, aiming down the sites. One of the two pirates appeared down the hall and Ander hesitated, waiting for the other to join him. The second the other target appeared, he pulled the trigger.

The gun bucked in his hand, firing a concentrated blast. Station weapons fired pulse blasts incapable of penetrating the outer walls but more than sufficient to kill when set to high power. Ander left his set to max. When the blast struck its target, the man screamed in pain and flopped on the ground, his ribs liquified.

The other, it turned out to be Rodent, looked down in shock and went to raise his weapon. Ander fired again just as the barrel of Rodent's rifle passed his knees. The attack smacked into the pirate's shoulder, tossing him to the ground. Before he could sit up, Ander fired twice more, hitting him in the legs and stomach.

He advanced to check them, ensuring they were truly dead. Strong hands gripped him from behind, yanking him to the ground. Harvin pounded his face with two solid blows but Ander blocked the third. They struggled for a moment, trying to gain an advantage when Ander brought his knee up, colliding with Harvin's side.

The pirate grunted, flopping away from him. Ander spun, aiming his weapon but it got kicked out of his hand. They rose to their feet, squaring off for a brawl. Ander knew he didn't have time for a drawn out battle. He threw himself at his opponent, slamming his fist into Harvin's stomach and face.

Harvin quickly realized he was overmatched but even desperation didn't help him. He got a lucky blow to Ander's side but when they grappled, the fight went to Ander. He pulled the pirate to the ground and got a good hold around his neck, squeezing with all his might. Harvin struggled, kicking his legs but a loud pop made him stop.

Panting, Ander didn't let him go for several moments, not until he believed the man to be truly dead. He shoved the body away and looked around frantically, struggling to remember his plan. Bringing up the layout on his tablet, he found the nearest airlock. Not quite two hundred yards away.

The bodies proved to be more difficult to drag than he thought and by the time he got them all there, Ander felt like he'd been exposed for far too long. He worked the controls to jettison the bodies all while inserting an error in the log stating the seal malfunctioned. This would lead people to believe the three men checked out a disturbance and were sucked into space.

It would buy Ander time to get back to his little cubby base with the supplies he needed.

The sound of air sucking through the door made him shiver, especially as he considered what exactly was happening to the bodies as they entered the vacuum of space. Such a tactic went against his conscience, why he left the military in the first place but such things couldn't matter just then. Survival and everyone on board took precedence over his peace of mind.

Three down, he thought, while gathering up food and water. Fates know how many to go. I need a tally…that'll be my next project. Get the cameras online and count them. I hope help gets here soon. I can only keep this up for so long.

Chapter 4

Rathe cursed under his breath as he watched the long range scanner. "Thantis," he called, "I'm picking up something big. Confirm?"

Thantis sighed and turned away from what he was doing. He remained silent for a moment before clearing his throat. "Yeah, I see it...but that's not an Alliance ship."

"Who the hell..." Rathe squinted at the screen. A moment of recognition hit him and his eyes went wide. "My God...that's the Behemoth."

"The what?" Thantis asked.

"The Behemoth. Earth ship. They built it in response to the attack a few years back. It's the most advanced vessel ever to be built by humans."

"So what?" Thantis shrugged. "Use the battleship to take it out."

Rathe glared at him. "Are you an idiot? That ship isn't some push over merchant we can muscle out of the system. That's a real warship captained by a man who knows war. If we attack them, they very well might put us down. Even if we win, it'll be a long shot. I mean, I'm good at tactics but those are trained professionals."

"So what do you suggest?" Thantis sneered. "Do you want to surrender?"

Rathe refrained from hitting the man but he really wanted to. He'd begun to seriously dislike the computer expert. Considering their situation, Thantis seemed entirely too cavalier. Hostages didn't guarantee an outcome. In fact, they usually just complicated things. Now, they might well be the bargaining chips that would save their lives.

"I'm going to talk to them," Rathe said. "And buy us some time to get everything loaded up for departure. You make sure that happens. I'm relying on you."

Thantis smiled and the expression made Rathe uncomfortable. "I'll have to head down to the reactor level. The computers have a direct access connection to what we need. It'll be faster."

"Great, fine. Go." Rathe waved his hand. "Do you need an escort?"

"I've got it." Thantis picked up a gun and limped toward the door. "I'll let you know when we're ready to fill the cargo containers."

"Just don't wait too long." Rathe turned to the controls, waiting for the hail from the Behemoth. He knew it would come soon and he had to be ready. Taking a deep breath to calm his nerves, he took heart in the fact that they wouldn't start firing on the station. His crew might not be willing to call their bluff.

Hell, I'm not sure I'd be willing myself...Keep cool. This is going to work out.

***

"Jump successful, Captain," Redding announced. "We have arrived...less than ten-thousand kilometers away from our mark."

"Outstanding work, Mister Collins," Gray said, making Timothy grin.

Olly cleared his throat, "I've got the Alliance ship on scans. She's got defensive shields up hot but her weapons are on standby. They don't seem to be reacting to us."

"Yet," Adam muttered. "Raise shields and go weapons hot, just in case."

Gray turned to Ensign Agatha White, the communications officer. "Agatha, get them on hail. Let's see if they want to have a talk."

"Aye, sir." Agatha paused a moment. "They're responding…they want to talk."

Gray nodded. "Put them on speaker." She nodded at him and he spoke into his microphone. "This is Captain Atwell of the USS Behemoth. We are here to negotiate the release of your hostages and to relieve you of Alliance property. Please reply."

"Can't do that, Captain Atwell." The male voice piping through the speakers carried a gruff tone to it. "We're not done with our task."

"If you're here just to steal Ulem, then I've got bad news for you," Gray said. "No one's going to buy it from you. We'll put out messages to every space port in friendly range. It'll be a waste of your time."

"We sell to anyone, Captain," the pirate said. "Even your enemies. Money's money to us."

Gray frowned. "Really. So you're not just a criminal but a traitor to your species as well. How long do you think that's going to work out for you?"

"It's worked pretty well so far. Look, we won't hurt the hostages if you just stay put. Once we're done loading up our vessels, you can do what you want. Have it back. I don't care but before you get it, we're going to leave here rich. Do you understand?"

"Perfectly." Gray muted the line. "Are the marines ready to depart?"

Adam nodded. "Yes, sir."

"Olly, jam their scanners," Gray said. "Make it look like something natural."

"I might be able to use the satellites to mess up their electronics." Olly hummed. "They're set up to amplify communications around the system, to allow the control center to talk to the deepest mining shaft on the planet. That means their transmitters are impressive but delicate. It wouldn't be beyond the realm of possibility for them to malfunction and trash their scans."

"Won't that mess up ours too?" Adam asked.

"No, sir. I'll compensate accordingly. Give me a moment."

"The moment he brings their scanners down, get those marines out there. I want the shuttle ready to board the station right away." Gray made the microphone live again. "So you're just here for the Ulem, huh? No ransom for the people you've taken?"

"Ransom's too messy," the pirate said. "No one's got time to mess with that kind of thing. You never get what you ask for anyway."

"Fair enough. What about that Alliance battleship? You can't honestly think I'm going to let you keep it."

"So what're you going to do? Blow it up?"

"If it means keeping it out of your hands," Gray replied, "then yes. Why should I let you roam around space terrorizing people? Sure, we need it for the war effort but we can't have a band of blood thirsty raiders chipping away at our backsides either."

"I should be insulted."

"If you'd like to be," Gray said. "But regardless of your feelings, we're going to work something out. A lot of you do not have to die today. It's really up to you."

"Let me think about it. Your offer, while incredibly generous...and by that I mean not at all, just doesn't seem like it'll set with my crew. However, we've got some time to kill so I'll get back to you soon."

"Don't make it long," Gray warned. "We're not entirely patient."

"Neither are we, believe me."

The line went dead and Gray stood up. "Clea, get to work on what we can do with that ship. Olly, how's that jam coming?"

"Almost done, sir." Olly scowled. "I essentially have to put the satellites on a timer and bust them after a period of time. If they just suddenly break, it'll be obvious we did it. However, I am making it clear that our entry into the system had to be the cause. The jump wake could easily be blamed."

"I don't think we're taking that ship whole," Adam said. "We might want to engage."

"Not yet," Gray said. "There may be Alliance crew onboard. I want to at least try to liberate it before we blow it out of the sky. Besides, as the pirate said, we've got some time. Let's explore some options. I'm sure we can make something happen."

***

Rathe leaned back in his chair and let out a deep breath. Earth military would be a lot more aggressive than the Alliance ever managed. When they felt like attacking, they'd come in hard and leave no survivors. If anyone surrendered, they'd spend the rest of their lives in prison. Anyone on his crew who knew that would fight to the death.

"Captain?" Jordan's voice crackled over the speakers. "You might want to come down here to the promenade. I...found something."

"Bad?" Rathe asked.

"Bad enough. Better hurry."

Rathe cursed and left the control center, jogging down the hallway. When he emerged, he saw several of his men standing at one end of the promenade, examining an airlock. He approached, scanning the area suspiciously. Jordan came closer to meet him, a tall man with thick black hair and a short beard.

"Glad you could make it so fast," Jordan muttered.

"What's going on?" Rathe asked. "What're you all doing over here?"

"Take a look." Jordan gestured to a smear of blood on the seals around the airlock. He tapped the console to bring up the logs. "It seems the seal malfunctioned and it shows three people were sucked out into space."

"How could a seal suck people out?" Rathe asked. "Surely the breach had to be bigger to do that. Who's missing?"

"Harvin, Nichols and Temmer."

"They're just gone?"

Jordan gestured to the airlock. "Apparently for good."

"God damn these mining facilities!" Rathe paced away. "How do we know the thing won't malfunction again? How'd it even close?"

"Automatic repair systems kicked in," Jordan explained. "Apparently, it was due for maintenance two weeks ago."

"Lazy bastards!" One of the other pirates muttered. "Got our boys killed! I say we find the maintenance men and throw them out the airlock!"

"Settle down." Rathe scowled. "We're not killing anyone, not with a battlecruiser breathing down our necks. They're just looking for a reason to come in here and kill us all. So keep your cool or we're all done."

"What do you mean battleship?" Another crewman stepped forward. Rathe didn't know him personally but had seen him around. Beady, blue eyes, shaved head, dusty facial hair…he'd struck him as a bit of a whiner. "From the Alliance?"

Rathe shook his head. "Worse. Earth."

"Damn it…" Jordan breathed. "What're we going to do?"

"I've stalled them for now. Thantis is getting the system ready to load us up quicker. Hopefully, we've got all the Ulem ready?"

"Our men have been packing it up since we arrived," Jordan said. "We should be good."

"Excellent. I'll keep the Earth ship from bothering us you guys focus on keeping this place secure. We'll be out of here soon and rich enough to retire if we're smart about it. So stay calm, right?"

The others agreed and went about their business but Jordan walked with Rathe back toward the control center.

"I'm concerned about this place," Jordan kept his voice low. "It's too big to have locked down completely. There might be a whole pocket of people we didn't find."

"Didn't you go over the personnel records?"

"Not entirely, they're long."

Rathe rubbed his eyes. "Lord, Jordan. Do it right. Get the personnel records and take a roll call. If we're missing someone, we need to know. Start with the security people if you can. They're the only ones we have to really worry about. The rest of these miners aren't exactly dangerous, right?"

"Yeah, I'll get on it…but it'll take a while."

"Then stop stalling and move out." Rathe shook his head. "Anymore mistakes like that and we might as well all throw ourselves out of airlocks. I'll be in the control center. Let me know if you find anything."

***

Ander's checkpoint gave him access to a wide variety of security stations throughout the facility. He picked up the entry of the Earth ship just as it arrived and when the pirates found the 'malfunctioned' airlock, he covertly tapped into the communication center there, listening to every word.

They bought my malfunction trick. Thank the fates!

He wanted to scan the facility to gain a good idea of the numbers they were facing, how many pirates they had to deal with but it had to be subtle. If someone caught on, they could trace his signal and then, he'd be done. The bolder his tactics became, the better chance he had of discovery and ultimately, he greater his chance of dying.

The Earth ship is here. Let them take control of the situation. They've got this.

But Ander didn't want to give up completely. He knew he could help them somehow. Even if he had to abandon his checkpoint and hide out somewhere else, he needed to grant them some intelligence. His mind made up, he initiated the facility wide scan, telling the computer to generate a report of all unauthorized personnel aboard.

A bar appeared at the bottom of the screen showing a percent completed. It indicated five minutes before it finished. Providing no one was paying attention in the control center, it would be finished before they could stop him. The pirates didn't seem to be entirely prepared to occupy the station properly, they just wanted to steal.

That gave Ander a small advantage.

Even military forces had a hard time occupying unfriendly territory, especially when the space was big. This station was no different. They didn't know it as well and that meant there were plenty of places to hide. If the security forces hadn't folded, they might've been able to take the station back but they proved gullible.

Buying that the pirates would destroy the station made no sense. Why jump into a sector only to blow up the only thing of value there? The risk and time wasted would never fly for any resource conscious group and criminals had to worry about where they'd find fuel, armaments and supplies.

Ander considered the situation. The next step involved reaching out to the Earth ship in a way that was private. A coded channel would work but voice might require too much bandwidth to cover up. Ander snapped his fingers. He could use one of the local satellites to bounce a signal, enabling voice with a slight delay.

Tapping at the console, he cursed under his breath. The satellites appeared to be offline...no, malfunctioning. Wow, can this get any worse? Back to the coded message method I suppose.

Ander drafted a simple message: security officer reaching out to Earth vessel. I am attempting to gather intel. Please respond. I'll have data soon. Once he finished, he encoded it and hit send. The computer calculated it would be received in less than ten minutes. How long it took them to get back to him entirely depended on their tech officer.

I hope he's a good one...None of us has time for anything less.

Ander sat back and tried desperately not to fret. Everything he could possibly do was underway. Waiting, painful as it felt, was his only course of action. He watched the percentage bar of his scan and willed it to hurry. The act wasn't productive but it kept him busy for the several minutes he needed to sit idle.

***

Olly finished his task and watched as the satellites appeared offline. A moment later, they began jamming scans in the area. He already programmed their equipment to compensate. Once he confirmed the station was down, he triple checked his work. A lot of lives were on the line and he didn't want sloppy work to get them killed.

"Captain, I've taken their scans offline," Olly announced. "The satellites are working as expected. If they have someone on board that can fix them, they might be up in an hour or so...but I doubt they can do it remotely. I don't even know if I could at this point."

"Great work," Gray said. "Launch those marines. Have them hit the facility immediately."

Commander Everly began giving the order when Agatha spoke up. "Oliver, I'm picking up a strange transmission from the station...it seems to be a coded text message. Can you confirm before I accept it?"

Olly tapped away at the console. A coded text message came through, a hastily packaged one at that. He scanned it for any malicious software and it showed clean. "Looks okay to me," he said. "Can you decode it?"

"Easily," Agatha replied. "Give me a moment..."

He turned and watched her work, her fingers flying over the console with practiced ease. A moment later, she scowled at her screen then turned toward the rest of them. "Captain, I've received a coded message from a security officer on the station. They say they're trying to gather intel for us and they'd like a response."

Gray turned to Adam. "The insider."

Adam nodded. "Better answer him."

"Go ahead and acknowledge the transmission and let him know that we're waiting for any more information." Gray paused. "Have him identify himself. I want to make sure we're talking to someone who is actually on our side."

"I find it unlikely that the pirates would try such a tactic," Adam said. "I mean, do you really believe they'd try to fool us with this kind of transmission? And how would they know about the insider unless…he…got caught…"

"Exactly," Gray replied. "We'll need a way to verify that he's not been broken. Olly, can you get on our briefing information and work with Agatha to find a way to verify this guy? I'd like to be open but we can't be stupid about it."

"On it, sir." Olly brought up the files on Ander Yin'Dran. The man fought for the Alliance for a long while. His service record. They wouldn't have quizzed him about that. If he's being held hostage, we can ask about his commanders. Someone random. If he answers right, we should be able to trust him. "I'm sending you something, Agatha. Ask him about his second CO."

"Got it," Agatha replied. "Sending challenge back now. I'll let you know when I've received the answer."

"Clea," Gray said, "how're you doing on the battleship?"

"I can't get a solid connection through their shields," Clea said, "but I did get the computer to send me a status. They don't seem to have modified it at all. Once I get our sensors tuned properly to break through their defenses, I should be able to take control. However, this status update is pretty old...it doesn't prove I won't run into obstacles."

"Work with Olly as you need to," Gray said. "Are the marines in motion yet?"

"They are, sir," Adam said. "But I think we should only get them close. If this security guard can help at all, he might pick a good place for them to board."

"Agreed. Agatha, let us know when we can trust that guy." Gray returned to his seat. "I want this place locked down as soon as possible."

"Revente is requesting permission to launch fighters," Adam announced. "They've been on ready thirty. Might help if we get them out there just in case."

"Do it quietly," Gray said. "Keep them close to the ship. I don't want to escalate this engagement."

Olly went back to work, ensuring the satellite malfunction kept the sensors down. The enemy wouldn't be able to pick up the fighters outside visual and the Behemoth was far enough away to make that unlikely. Still, he wanted to stack things in their favor to the best of his ability. He sent out massive sensor sweeps, immense energy scans which should look like the Behemoth was attempting to overcome the satellite malfunction.

At least that way, it would seem like they weren't responsible for blinding the station. Hopefully, the marines would make short work of the attack and they'd have the place locked down before it mattered.

After his time on the Tam'Dral and what happened on the research facility, he had confidence.

It was just a matter of time.

Chapter 5

Jordan burst into the command center. "All our sensors are down," he said. "The damn satellites malfunctioned and are causing total havoc on all our systems. We've been hit hard by this. Both our ships are reporting the same issue."

"Would it affect the Earth ship too?" Rathe asked. "Or I assume you think they had something to do with it."

"Probably," Jordan said, "on both counts. They SHOULD be impacted...honestly, there's enough evidence to suggest the satellites were overwhelmed by their jump. I was able to get the last diagnostic log from the things and some key components were damaged. Their tech person would have to be pretty amazing to make something like that happen."

"I wouldn't put it past them." Rathe cursed. "Okay, let me reach out and see what's going on."

He hit the button and tried to hail the Earth vessel, hoping they wouldn't hear the anxiety in his voice. "Listen up, we have some demands."

Captain Atwell answered him a moment later, "what changed your mind?"

"We've got some time to kill so why not ask for a few things? We want ransom for these people. A lot of it. I know you've got spare parts on board. Send some of them over. Specifically, for your pulse engines. We need them for our own ship."

"Out of the question," Captain Atwell replied. "Besides, I doubt you'd let us drop them off in your hangar anyway."

"Just jettison them. We'll pick them up after you leave."

"Or?"

Rathe hesitated. "We'll start killing the hostages."

"The moment one hostage dies, we take the station by force. We'll hit it with everything we've got and there won't be a single pirate left standing," Captain

Atwell paused for a moment, "how's that sound for a deal?"

Rathe muted the line and looked at Jordan. "These people are insane!"

"They probably mean it too. I've heard they don't negotiate well."

"I know for a fact they don't but I didn't think they'd get that hard." Rathe hummed. "I need to buy some time."

"Tell them that you'll give them a couple hostages in return for letting us pack our stuff up and leave." Jordan shrugged. "That'll be easier to get than any ransom."

"I like it." Rathe took the line off mute. "I've got a better idea. We'll release some hostages to you if you'll give us time to pack our ship up for departure. How's that?"

"When will you hand these people over?" Captain Atwell asked. "And how will they be delivered?"

"There're shuttles here," Rathe said. "We'll let a couple of hostages fly one over to you."

"Let me think about it." Captain Atwell killed the line and Rathe cursed again.

"That means they're trying to do something besides work with us," Rathe muttered. "What're we going to do?"

"Hurry," Jordan replied. "And get the hell out of here with as much booty as we can get. Where's that Thantis prick?"

"I don't know...I figured he'd be back by now."

"We'd better find him. He hasn't given us the automated loaders yet."

"Okay, but be careful. God knows what's going on in this place but I can tell you this: I already feel like it was a big mistake. For all we know, Thantis had an 'accident' like those others. I'm not interested in finding out what it's like to be sucked out of a damn airlock. Let's not add dying to our list of catastrophes."

***

Ander finished his scan of the station and let out a sigh of relief. There were thirty-six pirates on the station spread out through different parts. Most of them were relegated to watching the hostages but a large number gathered in the hangar where Ulem tended to be loaded up for shipping.

Then there was a lone pirate deep in one of the shafts built into the station. Long before Ander joined the crew, the station tethered a massive asteroid to the complex and had been mining it for a while. Supposedly, it had some of the richest deposits of Ulem ever discovered but it was dangerous down there. Because of the concentration of the element, miners had to be very careful. An explosion would be catastrophic.

Ander contemplated the screen, scowling at the news. What was one person doing down there? They couldn't take the raw materials straight from the walls and pirates sure weren't going to start mining. He had to find out but before he could, he needed to talk to the Earth ship.

They wrote back to him and asked who his second CO was. Ander smiled at the memory and replied to them that it was a man named Grissem Hin'Dahl. He also included the number of pirates they were facing and let them know he needed to check on something. Though the man might just be slacking off and trying to find a place not to work, Ander figured it was something much more nefarious.

He sent his message and left his station, letting his gun lead the way. Luckily, the shaft was close to his position, or at least, relatively so. He could take a ladder down two floors then hurry down a hall to the entrance. From there, he wouldn't even have to go inside to see what was going on. The security cameras would do the rest.

Ander slid down the ladder and jarred his ankle when he landed. Luckily, he was able to walk it off after a few steps but the fear he'd injured himself kept his heart racing as he began down the tunnel. This part of the station always creeped him out. The darkness felt oppressive and he heard the creaking of metal from what he imagined was extreme strain on the frame of the mine.

No one was around as he arrived at the massive door, which had been closed. The person inside must've known how to handle the computers if he pulled that off. Ander tapped into the security console and used his password. An image appeared on the screen of a man working on one of the mining machines, attaching something to its frame.

He zoomed in and gasped. Though he hadn't seen that particular variety, he knew the man was planting a bomb. A quick scan indicated he'd already planted several. He plans to blow up the entire facility! Is this what the pirates want? To cover their escape or something? It makes no sense!

Why waste all those resources? And how could they justify murdering all the hostages? Ander needed to get the Earth personnel aboard as soon as possible to stop this insanity. If they didn't get there soon, there'd be countless dead, families! Ander rushed back to his security station as fast as he could, panting as he typed in a new message.

They'll get this one after the last but better late than never...and they have to hurry. Hell, I need to find a good entry point for them. Ander started scanning the station for a boarding solution, somewhere they could gain a foothold without having to engage in a firefight. Then we can clear this place of those bastards...and stop them from blowing up my home.

***

"Commander?" Agatha grabbed Adam's attention and he turned to face her.

"What've you got, Ensign?"

"Response from the security officer," Agatha replied. "He answered the challenge question properly and he gave us a number of pirates. He claims there are thirty-six aboard. There's another part here...says he's going to check something out. That's all I've got from him so far."

"Thank you." Adam turned to Gray. "Seems we can trust him."

Gray nodded. "Okay. Now we need to know where to bring our men. They can get in undetected but the hangar's no good. The pirates will be there. They'll have to cut their way in…"

"Maybe not, Sir," Olly interjected. "The station has a variety of airlocks throughout for maintenance. I'm sure we can use one of those."

"Good call. We just need to know which one is safe then." Gray turned to Clea. "Any luck with the battleship?"

"Some…but not much." Clea shrugged. "It's going to be slower going than taking the station and I might add, I'm pretty sure we're going to have to engage them at some point. Even if I get in, they're going to have a minute to react and take action."

"Understood." Gray turned to Adam. "The fighters?"

"In position and ready to go." Adam checked his reports. "All stations report ready for combat. Were you serious about the threat you gave to the pirates?"

"Mostly," Gray said. "If they kill one hostage, they'll be willing to kill more and we can't sit around waiting for that to happen. Hopefully, we'll get in there and take them down before it gets to such a desperate state. Of course, we're getting close, right? They seem pretty rattled to me. Did you note the hesitation in the man's voice when he said they'd kill hostages?"

Adam nodded. "This might've gone beyond what they had in mind."

"I'm sure it has." Gray grinned. "Which gives us a slight advantage. They're not bloodthirsty butchers. Them exhibiting any humanity works for us."

"Sir," Agatha said, "I've got an update from Ander. He states that one of the pirates is attempting to sabotage the station. Apparently, the man attached some bombs to the delicate equipment in the reactor room. If they detonate, he believes the entire facility will be destroyed—the reactor will go and whatever Ulem is around will prove volatile as well."

Adam cleared his throat and turned to Gray. "So much for your theory about the pirates not being bloodthirsty."

"That was unexpected." Gray sighed. "I wonder why they'd risk such a gamble. What do they have to gain from blowing the facility up?"

"To cover their tracks?" Adam offered. "But we know what they're up to. It seems almost...I don't know...spiteful. Unnecessary."

"I agree." Gray hummed, rubbing his chin. "I'd like to get a better idea of who we're up against but these guys probably won't have records, at least not under whatever names we might get from them. I guess we're going to have to err on the side of them being murderous bastards but I really hoped they'd be more reasonable."

"What do you want to do?" Adam asked.

"Agatha, find out from Ander where to land our men. We'll clear it out and disarm the bombs as quickly as possible." Gray turned to Adam. "Give Marshall these new details. He'll want to know about the complication and I guarantee he won't be happy. This kind of thing gives him heart burn."

"I'm right there with him," Adam said as he tapped the com. "Let's just hope they can get this done in the time frame allotted."

"They don't have much choice," Gray said. "Get them briefed."

***

Rathe felt like the world around him was coming undone. Thantis missing, the loaders not even getting the Ulem aboard, people sucked out of airlocks, an Earth ship threatening to kill them all…what else could go wrong? He didn't want to ask the question out loud for fear it would be answered.

Then it was.

"Rathe? This is Hannah, come in."

He'd put Hannah in charge of the battleship while he was on the station. She proved to be a good ship officer and kept the men in line fairly well. Plus, she took to the systems quickly enough to know what to do when. Though they operated the vessel on the bare minimum number of people, she had it operating as efficiently as possible.

"Yeah, I'm here. What's going on? Please don't give me bad news…"

"'Fraid I have to. Our sensors are buggered but we have visual that the Earth ship launched fighters. They haven't engaged but I'd say we're close to having to deal with them."

"Damn it!" Rathe slapped the console. "They think they can just sneak around and get ready to attack us?"

"Probably. I'm pretty sure that's their whole point. Get us before we can do the hostages, right?"

"I'm not killing hostages," Rathe muttered. "But I think we can give them a little taste of some drones."

Jordan perked up at that. "Whoa, what're you talking about?"

"Attacking the Earth fighters with some drones," Rathe said. "It'll distract them."

"For how long, man? Then what? They're going to come down on us with some serious wrath! We can't take them if they direct all their attention on us."

"I beg to differ," Hannah said. "I've got the weapons hot on this thing. Let us blow them out of the sky. Then we'll have all the time in the world to get the Ulem. And I'd love to know what's taking you guys so damn long."

"We've got all kinds of complications," Rathe said. "But we're working them out. Jordan, do you honestly think they can't take the Earth ship?"

"I mean...I guess I can't say for certain they can't..." Jordan sighed. "It just seems pretty damn risky. If we were loading our stuff, I'd say go for it. But until we get those automated loaders up."

"What even happened to them?" Hannah asked. "Why were they down?"

"The bastards must've sabotaged them when we got here," Rathe said. "Thantis said they have special codes to start them up and he was trying to boot them back up. When he left, he went down to have a direct connection to make it faster."

"Find him then," Hannah said. "And I'm going to deal with our guest."

"Don't screw up, Hannah. If we lose that ship, we're screwed."

"We won't. Believe me." The line went dead.

"I hope she knows what she's doing," Jordan said. "For all our sakes."

"Definitely…" Rathe rubbed his eyes. We don't have time for all this nonsense.

***

Clea continued trying to hack the Alliance vessel, working through every code in the database. None of them worked so she resorted to alterations, tapping into the universal code to randomize her attempts. Whoever messed with the computer systems either really knew what they were doing or luckily destroyed the security setup.

Regardless, if began to frustrate her when suddenly the Alliance ship opened up and drones spilled out. She checked her scans and confirmed they were on their way toward the Behemoth.

"Captain," Clea tried to keep her tone calm but a slight tremor snuck in, "I believe we're being attacked."

"Confirmed!" Olly shouted. "Drones incoming!"

"Damn it," Adam grunted. "Revente, your pilots need to move! We've got drones incoming."

Gray scowled. "I'm shocked they attacked but while they are, get those marines moving. By the time they get there, hopefully we'll have a place for them to dock."

Agatha tapped away at her station and spoke up. "Ander has sent us coordinates. I'm providing them to the drop ship now."

"Good." Gray looked up at the view screen. "Let's make short work of those drones then we can bring those shields down. I hope you'll be ready to hack their computers soon, Clea. We're going to need to shut them off quickly."

"I'm working on it." Clea redoubled her efforts, frantically going through every program she had. Olly's work helped but only a little. She understood Alliance security better than most but it had changed quite a bit since she began working with the humans. Now, the gap between her knowledge and the present day caught up to her.

Maybe I'm going about this the wrong way. It's not Alliance security I should be attacking but low grade protocols. Something from the black market or even civilian sector. Those could be tricky compared to the military because they didn't have access to the same encryption. It's worth a try.

Clea tapped into a different database, one with every known non-military security protocol attached. She let the scan run and willed it to hurry. Combat was about to begin and it might not last long. As Gray said, her window may be a small one and if she had any hope of taking the Alliance ship intact, she needed to break in the moment the shields dropped.

***

Wing Commander Meagan Pointer leaned back in her seat and stared through the top of her canopy at the distant stars. They'd launched nearly fifteen minutes early and their engines sat on idle while they waited for orders. The pirates out there didn't bother her so much as the waiting. Pilots in general hated the long wait times.

"What do you think about these drones?" Squadron Leader Mick Tauran asked. He tended to fly on her wing and acted as her second in command. "I hear that's their primary fighter craft."

"I kind of doubt they're as good as the ones from the Tam'Dral," Meagan replied. She referred to their engagement in Earth space against the defense systems of a refugee ship. Those had been controlled by computers. "I guess there's a chance they might be unpredictable if people are at the helm."

"The maneuverability always worries me," Mick replied. "We can't pull those Gs."

"Won't matter. We have solid countermeasures and if we can cut the signal from pilot to craft, they drift. Easy lock & blow."

"That sounded dirty."

Meagan rolled her eyes. "Only to you, Mick."

"This is Giant One," Revente's voice crackled through the speakers. "We have drones incoming. You are ordered to engage, repeat...engage however, do not get too close to the Alliance battleship. It may open fire."

"Don't have to tell us twice." Meagan stretched her shoulders and grabbed her flight stick. "You heard the man, Panther Wing. Let's down some toy robots."

They departed in a loose formation, each ship far enough apart to give the drones some space. Meagan read about pirate tactics and they occasionally didn't mind sacrificing one of their ships to take out a piloted vessel. If one of their ships blew next to another, it could cause some serious collateral damage.

Radar picked up the enemy vehicles at extreme range. They were moving erratically, as if trying to foul up sensors. Meagan sent out a ping for an exact count but the computer brought back mixed results. She cursed under her breath. This might make for a long fight, especially since they had to be mindful of their surroundings.

Suddenly, one of the drones flew past them at extreme speed, little more than a blur on Meagan's right.

"Did you see that?" Meagan asked.

"Yeah, it didn't show up on my scans…" Mick replied.

"Nor mine," Panther Seven, Lieutenant Richard Martin, added. "It's circling around."

"Panthers Seven and Eight, engage that thing," Meagan ordered. "The rest of you break up into twos and prepare for a real fight. Tiger Wing is our back up so if you need some support, head back to the Behemoth. Time to go to work."

Meagan and Mick pulled away from the others. She climbed, he dove and they approached the swarm of drones. Maybe this'll be easier than I thought. She pulled the trigger for her pulse cannons, sending out bolts of light hammering into the tiny ships. A number of bulb explosions light up the sky then went dark.

An alarm went off in her cockpit as a torrent of blaster fire riddled her aft shields. Okay, maybe not as easy as I thought.

"I see it," Mick said. "Deploy your countermeasures and I'll take it out."

Meagan flipped a switch and two micro transmitters dropped from the bottom of her ship. When they hit vacuum, they sent out a strong burst signal, interrupting the sensors, and controls, of the pursuing drone. As it drifted in a straight line, Mick blew it out of the sky and formed up beside her.

"Where'd that thing come from?" Meagan asked but there was no time to find out. Another five of them started hammering at her shields and she jammed her throttle forward. The sudden increase in speed pressed her into her seat and she still didn't put any appreciable distance between her and the unmanned attackers.

"They're all over us!" Panther Five shouted out, Lieutenant Leslie Eddings. "Tiger Wing, we need some help over here!"

"Engaging," someone on Tiger Wing called out but Meagan didn't recognize their voice. She had to concentrate on evasive maneuvers, trying to out fly the agile little bastards behind her. A thought crossed her mind but she really didn't like the odds of it. Still, considering Mick had his own problems it might be her best chance.

Meagan maneuvered toward the largest concentration of drones and once again buried her throttle. As she rocketed toward them, she began a countdown to contact. More blasts hammered her shields but they held, at least for the moment. When she had visual on the drones, she pulled up and hit the breaks. Her safety straps bit into her skin and the inertial dampeners whined loudly.

Two of the drones slammed into their buddies, exploding in a spectacular display. This caused a small chain reaction and she splashed at least four more for a grand total of six. It helped alleviate the immediate pressure but there were plenty more where that came from. All around her, the pilots fought off the attack. As her confidence began to build, she saw one of their own ships explode.

Oh God...who was that?

"Panther Wing, report in!" Meagan cried out, entering a spin and diving to void another torrent of fire. Her mind threatened to drift to the pilot they may have lost but she fought hard to keep her focus on flying. People's voices filled her speakers, each of her people finally sounding off.

Tiger Wing...that's awful. Damn it!

"I've got two..." Mick called out. "Never mind, they're done."

"Missiles away," Panther three shouted. "Direct hits!"

"I have an idea," Panther Four, Flight Lieutenant Shelly Brown said. "Instead of fighting these drones, let's take out their ability to control them on the alliance ship."

"Yeah, how're they flying anyway?" Mick asked. "I thought we took down all sensor contact."

"These things don't rely on sensors," Meagan replied. "They don't care about the satellite malfunction and they've got their own guidance systems. But we were given orders to avoid the Alliance ship."

"We could be fighting these things for an hour or more," Shelly said. "And who's to say we won't lose more pilots?"

Meagan fired a rocket and destroyed a drone, dove under the explosion and kicked her com over to command. "Giant Control, this is Panther One requesting permission to attack the Alliance battleship and destroy their ability to control their drones."

"Permission…" Giant control hesitated. "One moment."

"Now's not the time for holding," Meagan said, diving again as one of the drones attempted to suicide into her. "We're having some trouble out here and need to do something drastic."

"Just hold on, Panther One, I'm getting clearance."

Hurry the hell up! Meagan bit the words back and focused on staying alive. She tapped into her computer and had it start analyzing the battleship to find where the drone control was located. It might not be possible to take it out with the shields up but then again, they had some decent ordinance. The only thing they really had to do was nudge the thing, not even totally destroy it.

A little disruption would go a long way.

"How do you plan on taking it out, Panther One?" Giant Control asked. She explained they would use missiles when they got close enough and disrupt the signal. "You have permission to try but you'd better be damn careful. They have cannons on those things and they're good at homing in on targets if you know what I'm saying."

"Roger that," Meagan replied. "Panther Four, you got your wish. We're going in. Panthers Two and Three, you're with us. The rest of you remain behind and keep these things busy. We want as few targets around their ship as possible."

The four ships sped off, leaving behind the action. A couple of drones gave chase but the other members of Panther Wing made short work of them, giving Meagan's small team a chance to get into position.

Meagan's computer continued to scan the vessel and she really started to feel some pressure. If they didn't have a target before they got in range, they'd be screwed. No amount of prayer would save them from those cannons and flying around the battleship without a target would pretty much be suicide.

Finally, at extreme range, her computer found the source of the drone signal and painted the target on her HUD. She transmitted it to her other pilots. "That's what we have to hit…looks like they installed it near the top decks. Shouldn't be too bad…they're running shields on defensive but not full power. We might get lucky."

An alert sounded in her cockpit, warning her that the cannons went live on the ship. How'd they see us so quickly? Must be the corona from our thrusters…but I didn't anticipate they'd be so on it. Blasts from the ship filled the sky, giving them one more thing to dodge. As they hurtled toward their target, the extra challenge made it all the trickier.

"I've been hit!" Panther Three, Flight Lieutenant David Benning, called out through the com. "That cannon went right through my shields…I've lost my right maneuvering thruster."

"Get out of there!" Mick shouted. "Pull back and get to a safe distance!"

"I'm…" David paused. "Damn it, I have to bail out. The pulse engines on an over drive."

"Aim at the Alliance ship," Shelly said. "Hit your throttle then bail out."

"Done…"

Meagan glanced over her shoulder in time to see his life pod eject from the ship as it rocketed toward its destination. Cannons took some shots at it but they missed and a moment later, it splashed against their shields. When the pulse engine ignited, the explosion made Meagan wince and look away for a moment.

Readings indicated the shields weakened, giving them a better chance to damage the drone control center. "Get a good missile lock people," Meagan called. "We don't want to waste that resource."

They blanketed open space with projectiles and Meagan fired a few pulse blasts for good measure. As the last of her missiles left her craft, she spun around and dove, getting out of the firing arc of the turrets. The rest of her wing joined her, plunging away from the battleship and putting some distance between them and the explosion.

"We have to get David!" Shelly said. "He's closest to me, I'm on it."

"Tractor him back," Meagan said. "We'll cover you as best we can."

The missiles found their target. The first few made the shield light up but the firepower overwhelmed the defenses in that one area, enough so that the surface of the ship took some serious concussion damage. Something flashed on the battleship and a moment later, Tiger One crackled over their speakers.

"The drones stopped moving! You did it!"

"For now," Meagan said. "They can regain control so wipe them out as quickly as you can."

She looked back toward the Behemoth and watched several small explosions dot the horizon. Tiger Wing and the rest of Panther mopped up the final drones floating there lifeless in space. Shelly joined them, David's life pod following behind her. Meagan ran a quick scan and found a life sign and her shoulders relaxed.

"No response to hails," Shelly said, "but he's still alive in there."

"Ejecting at that velocity would've knocked anyone out," Mick said. "Let's get him to medical right away."

"Before they launch some real fighters," Meagan replied, "though I'd be happy to take them on after this nonsense. Drone flying cowards."

"You might get your wish," Giant control announced. "But for now, they seem to be standing down. All pilots, begin your rearm cycle. We might be in for a long night."

***

Chapter 6

Captain William Hoffner stood at the back of the drop ship as it lumbered toward the mining facility. His men, all armored up and ready for action, seemed unusually calm before this action. Normally, they got boisterous before a mission but today, they seemed almost placid. It didn't help they'd been on standby for the last thirty minutes.

"You guys okay with this?" Hoffner called out. "You sound like you're napping."

They shouted in unison and stamped a foot. Hoffner grinned. "That's better." They went over the recent intel and knew they were up against thirty-six pirates. Twelve heavily armed marines seemed more than sufficient to take them down and no one on board displayed an ounce of concern over the numbers.

Unarmored personnel against them would have a bad day.

Their weapons were loaded with special ceramic rounds designed specifically not to penetrate the hull of the facility. They'd certainly do a number on a human body though, to the tune of blowing out organs and taking off limbs with decent aim. Alliance tended to use beam weapons but the Earth soldiers kept to their projectiles.

The security guard contact aboard the facility gave them a good place to dock in one of the subsections, a place where visual would be impossible from the upper decks. They'd get aboard as quietly as possible and may even gain the element of surprise. Attacking the pirates when they least expected it would make short work of those men who were set to guard the hostages.

Then we take the command center.

When Hoffner heard about the bombs, he found the complication annoying but not out of hand. He had plenty of demolitions experts on his team and they could easily disarm the ordinance. It did speed up their timeline though. They needed to clear up the explosives before shooting or the criminals might blow the station in desperation.

Depending on where their leaders were, he wouldn't put it past them to sacrifice a few lackeys. Which led him to the next problem after the station: the battleship.

Another drop ship floated around out there waiting for a chance to board the cruiser. There was no way to know how many people were on that thing until Clea got into their systems properly. He didn't know how long it would take her but after she worked with him at the research facility, he had a lot of faith.

Still, his objective remained the facility so he tried to put the ship out of his mind. When they docked, they'd be nonstop busy but for the moment, he enjoyed the peace and quiet of a final approach. The pilot announced that they were less than five minutes out. Three hundred seconds to action…Here we go.

***

Clea worked feverishly when the pilots attacked the Alliance ship. When the shields flared from the fighter crashing into the surface of the vessel, she tried to gain access during the fluctuation. She didn't gain control but did manage to download a log file with all the system changes in the last month.

Better that than nothing, I guess. At least I can see what they did to our ship.

Someone, an actual computer specialist, had gone through and performed some heavy modifications to the programming. The safety codes, the ones Clea hoped to use to gain computer access, had not only been changed but completely abolished. There were no back doors anymore, just the front end...or at least, that's what the programmer wanted her to believe.

During her search, she found a single line mentioning his back end login, the place where he made all his changes from. Scrutinizing what little code she managed to get, she saw that he'd basically modified the back door then masked it to suggest he closed it up. Clever...but there's always evidence.

"Olly," Clea approached. "This guy knew computers but he seemed to think we wouldn't. I've found his backdoor. I need you to send me the Protocol Seven code."

Olly sat up straight. "I see what you want to do. That's...kinda brilliant."

"Thank you," Clea turned back to her tablet. "I'll need you to do a code check when I'm done. When I'm done, we should be able to hack their system while leaving the shields up...which should then take them completely by surprise when we start shutting systems down."

She tapped away, inserting the Protocol Seven code so that it would gently penetrate the shields, inserting her control code. Once she implanted her program, it would respond to her commands even through the defenses. It would be as if she sat behind one of their consoles with a mild delay.

Clea finished it up and sent it over to Olly, then turned to Gray. "Captain, I believe I'll have control of the

Alliance ship shortly. However, they will have the opportunity to stop my attempt if they're very on it."

"I suspect you're about to ask me for something?"

"Yes…I would like you to attack the ship. A simple engagement will do. Once you hit them a few times, they should be too distracted to notice my subtle computer attack. After that, I'll shut down their weapons and the marines can do their thing."

"Easy enough." Gray turned to Adam. "You heard the lady. On her mark, we attack."

"Fighters?" Adam asked. "Or just us?"

"Just us, I think," Gray said. "No need to risk pilots on those turrets but keep them out there in case they launch fighters. My thought is they'll try to stop any boarding party and we'll need our ships to run screens."

"I just received a report from Marshall," Adam said. "The marines are about to board."

"Great. Have them keep us informed of their progress as they can. I'm pretty sure they're going to be swamped once they get in there."

Clea smiled. "At least we're getting somewhere, right?"

"Absolutely," Gray said. "We'll take possession of both inside the next few hours. However, I'm still worried about the pirate's ship. Not the battlecruiser but they have to have a freighter, something they were flying around in before they commandeered that one."

"Probably what they'll try to escape in," Adam said. "Olly, can you find it?"

"If it's attached to the station, that's going to be tough." Olly hummed. "I'll try some things though, sir. Give me a minute…shouldn't take long."

***

Jordan stood up and slapped the computer console, cursing loudly.

Rathe glanced over his shoulder, brow furrowed. "What the hell? You got a problem?"

"Yeah, we didn't find Thantis yet but while our guys were scanning for him, we found a hot security station." Jordan shook his head. "Some prick is down there sending messages out from the station!"

Rathe sighed, rubbing his eyes. "Please tell me you're joking."

"You think I'd kid around about this? God knows what kind of information he's transmitted! We're probably screwed!"

"Settle down," Rathe said. "Just...get the guy and we'll find out what he gave them. It's no big deal, just send our guys down there. Hell, maybe he knows where Thantis is."

"Yeah, I'm sending some people alright. They're already on the same level so it shouldn't take long."

"Great," Rathe replied. "Just don't kill him. We need him alive, right?"

"Alive." Jordan nodded. "But not necessarily in one piece. Don't worry. We'll get him."

***

Ander watched his scanner, waiting for the Earth soldiers to get close enough for a subtle communication, something which wouldn't get picked up by the pirates. The few minutes it took drove him crazy and sweat formed on his face and his nerves made him tap his foot. When they came into range, he sent them a hail.

The pilot replied.

"This is Crate One responding. Who is this?"

"This is Ander Yin'Dran, facility security forces! I'm the guy who's trying to get you on board."

"Let me patch you through to Captain Hoffner." A moment passed and he heard a click in his ear.

"This is Captain Hoffner. You're the local contact?"

"I am!" Ander replied. "Thank you for taking my call! I see you received my message about where to dock."

"We should be there shortly," Hoffner replied. "Are you going to be ready to open the airlock?"

"I'll head out in just a moment but it's just around the corner. I'll have you board on the same level

I've been hiding out. We can get just about anywhere from here...with some effort."

"Perfect. You get us on board, show us around and we'll treat your home as respectfully as possible. I look forward to meeting you in person."

"You too." Ander stood, prepared to leave. "Yin'Dran out!" He killed their connection and bolted out the door...

...very nearly running into an armed man. He wore a ratty vest, a dirty gray sweater and cargo pants tucked into low boots. Ander hesitated for only a moment as they made eye contact. The pirate took a step backward and shouted, "I found the source of the signal! He's over here!"

Ander lashed out and grabbed the man's gun, turning it away from him. The weapon fired, the barrel searing his hands as the energy bolt splashed harmlessly off the hull. He didn't let go, weathering the pain as he threw a kick, connecting with the man's groin. The pirate cried out and crumpled to the ground, letting his weapon go.

Several people began running in their direction, their boots hammering the floor. Ander turned and ran for the airlock to let the soldiers in, sprinting as fast as his legs would carry him. He heard the guy he knocked down shouting for his buddies to chase after him, crying out that they needed to hurry.

Ander arrived at the airlock and peered out. Two windows, one on each door, provided a good view of the outside. He saw the drop ship approaching, closing in to link up with the facility. He turned his attention to the hallway and fired several shots at where the men were about to be. The energy blasts splashed into the walls, letting his pursuers know he meant business.

Someone returned fire and Ander ducked, pressing himself against the wall as tightly as possible. Making himself a smaller target helped but the criminals had more firepower. He counted at least four weapons firing at him. How did they find me? Damn it!

The floor trembled, just a vibration as the drop ship connected with the facility. Ander risked a look at the control panel and saw that the seal was firming up.

It needed twenty seconds to be ready for the doors to open. That's a lifetime! If they decide to charge me, this is over!

"Someone's docking!" A pirate shouted. "Is he at an airlock?"

"Stay back!" Ander shouted. "If you come around the corner, you're dead! I swear to the Fates, I'll blast you down one at a time if I have to!"

"He's bluffing! Let's rush him!" One of the pirates bolted out and Ander fired, hitting him square in the chest. The man screamed, flopped on the ground and expired a moment later, a couple twitches heralding the end of his life.

"Want to test me again?" The timer counted down to five. Almost there!

"There has to be a way around him," someone else shouted. "Get over there and flank him!"

The airlock chimed, indicating the seal was complete. Ander reached up and slapped the button to open it up another countdown started. This one started at ten but it still made him groan. He heard footsteps off to his right. If he remembered the area correctly, they needed to sprint to get to the other side in less than two minutes.

Regardless, he'd be cutting it close and he had no way to warn the soldiers what they were walking into. Worse, he had to survive the next several minutes. There were too many little things the men needed to know before they started their campaign to free the station. Ander aimed his weapon the opposite direction of where he shot the first man.

"We're in position!" Someone yelled.

"Give it up, security man!" The first guy called out. "We've got you surrounded and you don't have to die today!"

"If you want me, come get me!" The doors began to open. *Fates, I'm really hoping you're on my side here.*

Pirates advanced.

Ander took aim and silently said a prayer.

A criminal poked his head around the corner. Just as Ander planned to fire, another blast went off and struck his weapon, tossing it from his hands. He scrambled to draw his pistol when three people shouted at the same time, something to the tune of don't do it! He instead lifted his hands over his head...

And chaos broke loose.

Quick bursts of gunfire barked from the airlock and two of the pirates danced like fish out of water them dropped to the ground. A major firefight broke out with Ander ducking low and making himself small. People started shouting and screaming but though it seemed to go on forever, the entire situation must've lasted less than thirty seconds.

Someone started running off and a couple of the soldiers pursued. Ander looked up into the barrels of multiple guns, the armored carriers each wearing the same faceless helmet.

"I'm Ander Yin'Dran," he said quickly. "Please don't shoot!"

"Stand down," another man stepped forward, tapping his helmet so the face rose. He was definitely human, a rugged looking sort. He offered Ander a hand.

"I'm Captain Hoffner. Looks like we showed up just in time."

"I have no idea how they found me," Ander replied as he stood. "But they were hellbent on taking me alive."

"Probably to find out what you've seen and who you've talked to." Hoffner turned as the men returned dragging two bodies. "They didn't get far."

"They were nearly at the elevator when we got a good shot."

"Looks like we're down to thirty-one." Hoffner glanced at Ander. "So what's our top priority?"

"I don't know," Ander replied. "On one hand, I'd say clearing out the rest of the pirates and rescuing the hostages. However, we've got another problem too. Those bombs…they've been planted and I have no idea how long we've got to take care of them. Interestingly enough, they haven't been loading Ulem onto their ship."

"Why not?"

"The automatic loaders are down. Our people sabotaged them."

Hoffner grinned. "Detaining them here. Good thinking...for the product at least. But these bombs, they must be planning to cover their tracks though I'm surprised they'd want to kill their cash cow."

"If they got away with enough Ulem," Ander replied, "they wouldn't need a cash cow for a long time. Even the most extravagant spender would probably be good for life."

Hoffner nodded. "I see. Okay, so we have to preserve the station by taking care of those bombs. How many are there?"

Ander sighed. "I don't know...I couldn't get into the room. It's the reactor area and though there are access tunnels, they're pretty small. The main doors are huge to allow for parts and such to get in but those are sealed."

"Do you think they can be opened from the command center?"

"Absolutely." Ander nodded emphatically. "If we took that back, we'd have control of all the doors. Even the little security centers throughout the station don't have as much control."

"Okay, so we'll have to come back to those and hope they don't detonate until we can get in." Hoffner turned to the other marines. "We're going to need to clear this place along the way so be ready. I'm thinking the elevator is probably off limits so get ready for ladders." He turned to Ander. "Assuming access points are ladders?"

"Yes, I can get us to the promenade which has a direct connection to the command center." Ander gestured. "Just follow me but um…be warned. It's a longer climb than I anticipated the last time."

"Don't worry," Hoffner said. "We're used to things not being as easy as they should be. I'm going to send a message back to the Behemoth as we go. After that, let's make this quick. I think these hostages have been under the sway of criminals long enough."

***

Rathe sat forward and stared as the Behemoth fired up her engines and began to move. His heart sank as he realized what that must've meant. He gestured at Jordan to come see and the two men watched as the massive ship began moving toward their battleship. They could only be up to one thing.

"I should've known this was coming after they attacked the drone signal," Rathe muttered. "I shouldn't have let her attack them!"

"Notice the idiot didn't press her attack after the drones got taken out," Jordan said. "In fact, has she even called in?"

"No, and I'm half tempted to have her jump out of here before they take it." Rathe dialed her in on the communicator. "Hannah, do you see what we see?"

"Yes," Hannah snapped. "I'm a little busy right now."

"What happened to you blowing them out of the sky?" Rathe asked. "You didn't even attack with the cannons!"

"The drones should've been more effective! How did I know they'd take out the control station?" Hannah cursed. "They're moving in to engage. I have to go if I hope to fight these bastards off!"

"Or," Rathe said, "you could jump out of here and keep our prize!"

"I'm not running from a bunch of Earth scum. No way. These guys are going to die."

"They already proved to be a hard target," Jordan said. "Why continue to indulge bad luck and have them really show you what they can do?"

"You two keep getting the Ulem," Hannah said. "And I'll handle ship operations, okay?"

"You're going to wind up dead!" Rathe shouted, slapping the console. "I'm ordering you to stand down and get the hell out of here!"

"And I'm telling you to get stuffed. I've got this." Hannah killed the connection and Rathe lost his mind for a moment. He kicked over a chair, slapped the wall and let out a string of profanity that would've made the hardest man blush before finally regaining his composure. Jordan watched him, staying out of the way.

"I'm better now," Rathe said, panting.

"You sure?" Jordan asked. "You want to go shoot someone?"

"Yes, Hannah." Rathe pointed vaguely behind him. "Moron's about to lose something we all fought very hard to attain!"

"I guess we have to just have some faith." Jordan tapped at one of the tablets. His expression turned grave. "Damn it."

Rathe groaned. "What now?"

"The men I sent to find that security guard aren't reporting back," Jordan said. "Their coms are up but they don't answer. That's...bad."

"You think?" Rathe shouted, putting his hands on his head. "I swear, this was a doomed venture! We never should've thought we could take a facility this large and turn it around!"

"Pull yourself together, man! That one guy might've taken down our five but we've still got a decent force on here. What do you think is going to happen? You think he might come up here and kill us? Ridiculous! We'll just lock the door!"

Gunfire made them both freeze. They exchanged glances. "Was that…" Rathe whispered.

Jordan nodded. "In the promenade."

"Can we get eyes down there?"

"The bastard must've freed some hostages somehow." Jordan shook his head. "This is crazy!"

"I'm sure it gets worse, Jordan. That's what this job is constantly doing: going from worse to even worse…I'm a little over it."

"Hold on…I'm picking something up." Jordan paused. "What is going on…"

Rathe took a deep breath and waited for more bad news.

***

"Distance to target," Gray asked aloud.

"Extreme range of weapons," Timothy answered. "Closing fast."

"I'll have good lock in less than thirty seconds," Redding added. "Olly, get me some targets. I'd like to pinpoint a few locations…non destructive, just enough to give them a heart attack."

"On it." Olly hummed. "We have to avoid some locations…feeding the targeting computer now and…you're good."

"Increasing speed," Redding said. "On your mark, Captain, we'll begin the engagement."

"Fighters report ready for screens," Adam offered. "They're with the marines now."

Agatha piped in, "Captain Hoffner just reported in. They are on board the station and moving to clear the command center. He states there's a situation with bombs but they need access to take care of it."

Gray nodded. "Sounds like most things are going according to plan. Redding, you have permission to engage. Let's return this thing to its rightful owners…just a little worse for wear."

Redding fired and pulse blasts hammered the Alliance starship. Shields bloomed as they defended against the assault, flaring as they nearly overloaded. "Olly, is there something wrong with their defenses? I wouldn't have thought to see that on our first blast."

"It seems our weapons are super loading them," Olly replied.

"Part of what I'm doing," Clea said. "The Protocol Seven code has dramatically weakened their shields. You won't need to fire for much longer. I've almost got control of their vessel. Just another moment..."

Olly sat up straight, "sir, they're launching fighters! Um...real fighters this time, not those drones!"

"Adam, let our people know to engage those fighters and take them down," Gray said. "Then get that drop ship moving. Once their weapons are down, I want to have boots on their decks in five."

"On it, sir." Adam got in touch with Revente and gave the orders.

"Give them one more pass," Clea said. "Different targets to avoid damage. I need thirty seconds for this to be complete…"

"You sure they won't detect you?" Gray asked.

"They won't if they keep trying to avoid being blown up," Clea said. "I'm hoping shipboard pulse cannons are a higher priority than a flashing computer console. Of course, they might not even know what the indicator means in which case this attack would be unnecessary but I've learned a saying from you. Better to be safe than sorry."

"And we drew out their fighters," Adam said. "That's a win right there."

"Less people to deal with for the marines." Gray nodded. "Okay, let's wrap this up then."

Olly grunted. "Sir, we've got a problem."

"What is it?"

"It looks like they've decided they'd rather not give up their prize." Olly brought his readings up on the screen. They saw a schematic glowing green. "This indicates a core overload."

Gray stood up. "Are they trying to blow the damn thing up themselves?"

Olly nodded. "Yes, sir. They've got it set to self destruct."

Gray turned to Clea. "Can you shut that down?"

"I'll try…but I might only be able to slow it. If they set it manually, the marines will have to take care of it."

"Time to detonation?" Gray asked.

"Less than ten minutes," Olly said. "And sir, when that thing goes so close to the station…it's going to take a serious chunk with it."

"Damn it…" Gray rubbed his eyes. "Tell the pilots to hurry. Get those shields down, Clea. We need those men on board five minutes ago. Let's focus, people. This mission just went from going easy to working hard and I'll be damned if we let that ship go because they're a bunch of sore losers."

Chapter 7

"Rathe, I think we have a serious problem!" Jordan shouted. "What the hell is Hannah doing?"

"What're you talking about?" Rathe looked at his companion's screen and cursed. "Is that what I think it is?"

Jordan nodded. "It sure as hell is!"

Their ship's energy build up remained consistent with a core going critical or, more likely, a self destruct sequence. Hannah got what she wanted: the Earth ship attacked but instead of taking them down, she folded. Rathe hit the com and hailed the ship which it connected immediately.

"What do you want?" Hannah asked, sounding as calm as if she was just taking a turn around a moon.

"What do I want?" Rathe's tone oozed exasperation. "You insane bitch! Stand down from that explosion and jump out of here!"

"I can't," Hannah replied. "They got into our computer somehow. The shields are coming down. The only thing they can't do is stop my self destruct...not through a damn computer. And I'm about to ram this thing down their throat. They'll be gone in a minute, Rathe and then you'll owe me one."

"You're very noble," Rathe sneered. "All the Ulem we get won't be worth losing that ship! Now shut it down!"

"They'll take this thing if I do, you know that right?" Hannah clicked her tongue. "No, kiss this sucker goodbye. I'm out."

"No!" Rathe slapped the console. "Hannah! Hannah, come in! Did she..." He turned to Jordan. "Did she really just cut us off?"

Jordan nodded slowly, his expression one of resignation.

"Get someone else on the com! Um...crap! Who...oh! Contact Aris! He can stop her!"

Jordan didn't move and Rathe reached past him, hitting the com. "Aris! Get your ass on this line now! Aris!"

No one connected. The line remained dead. Rathe felt helpless as he tried other people on the ship. He got nothing but static. Turning to the view screen, he watched as the Earth ship moved forward. Their own stolen ship stopped firing their cannons. *I guess they figure there's no point in firing anymore...wait!*

"What's that?" Rathe pointed. Jordan finally looked up and smirked.

"Wow...Hannah launched fighters. I'll bet she's amongst them. There's little chance that selfish bitch would let herself die."

"She'd better pray to whatever divinity she believes in I don't ever find her," Rathe clenched his fist. "So what's going on in the promenade?"

"Looks like a gunfight." Jordan shrugged helplessly. "God knows who with but those are projectile weapons, not energy. Did the Earth ship board us?"

"Probably." Rathe rubbed his eyes. "Come on, let's get Thantis and beat him to death. Then we'd better get the hell out of here. This mission's pretty much scrapped."

***

Meagan and four of her wing escorted a drop ship as it headed for the Alliance cruiser. Giant control reached out to her, requesting a secure channel. That's a bad sign. She connected, bracing herself for bad news.

"This is Panther One, go ahead."

"Meagan," Revente said. Even worse sign. He never uses my first name. "I've got a bad update. There's trouble."

"Just say it."

"The pirate bastards set the ship to overload. It's going to blow shortly. Couple that with the fact that they sent out fighters to stop you from delivering your payload."

"So what's the damage if it goes up?"

"Your shields won't save you…"

"What's the idea then? Get back?"

"No, we need that drop ship to get on board. We can still save it if we get some people in there."

"Sounds like a ridiculous risk," Meagan said. "Why aren't we pulling back and letting it go?"

"Because it's part of the mission…" Revente sighed. "But you'd better hurry…we don't have time to debate it."

"God damn it." Meagan hummed. "How many fighters am I taking on?"

"We've got ten. Tiger Wing can't get there in time either."

"I admire your confidence…I guess. Thanks, Giant Control. I don't like you much right now."

"Understood, Meagan. I'll see you soon."

Megan switched over to her people and let them know what was happening. "I wouldn't blame any of you if you were pretty pissed off at me right now."

Panther Three, David Benning spoke up. "Nah, this is what I signed up for. Besides, I'm pretty sure we've got this."

"More confidence," Meagan said. "Anyone else got something to say?"

"We've got your back," Mick said. "Let's go."

Meagan's scans picked up the incoming fighters. They were on a course for the drop ship. She gunned her throttle, on a course to meet them head on and before they could start taking potshots at her charge. The computer did a quick assessment and she felt a little better about the fight.

Their opponents were practically flying antiques. Superior firepower would chew through them. It came down to their skills as pilots. Panther wing just had to keep away from direct fire while the pirates wouldn't even survive a graze. Of course, if their objective was solely to prevent the marines from landing or even just to delay them…That would be possible.

I can't believe these guys are willingly committing suicide to blow up that ship. It's insane.

"Panther Three and Four, stay with the drop ship while Two and I take the fight to them," Meagan announced. "With any luck, we'll break their group up enough to where you'll get the really dedicated ones. Drop ship, get your turrets ready. There's a lot of them out here."

She received a series of acknowledgements from her people just as she and Mick got within range. The computer indicated she had seconds before she'd have to move aside or ram one of the pirates. Her finger twitched on the trigger, warming her cockpit and unleashing a barrage of fire on the incoming vessels.

Something exploded but she didn't have time to see what. Pressing her stick forward, she took her ship into a quick dive then immediately leveled out, maneuvering to get behind the pirates. Her scans showed one of the enemy trying to get her six but another blip appeared, her wingman.

Mick blew the pirate away and veered off to tend to his own problems.

Meagan's shields flared on the starboard side and she performed a barrel roll then changed course. Her attacker tried to mirror her move but the inertial dampeners must not have been as good. It flailed for a moment but was only half way through its turn when Meagan took it down.

Other explosions sounded behind her and she noted that some of the pirates made it to the drop ship. Spinning around, she raced back in time to see three more enemy ships blown away by Panther Three and Four. Mick flew by her at an insane speed, with two fighters hot on his tail.

Meagan gave pursuit, falling in behind them and firing a blast. Mick seemed to instinctually climb enough to avoid the friendly fire but she missed with her first shot. The second caught one of her targets on the rear engines. The thrust immediately went out and the pilot bailed just before their craft disintegrated.

The other one fired a missile, a slow lumbering thing. Mick fired off countermeasures and climbed, letting the ordinance explode harmlessly in the midst of his defenses. Meagan took another shot but her prey dodged the attack. Lord, this guy's actually good!

"What are you doing back there, Meagan!" Mick called out. "Can you take this guy down or what?"

"It's not as easy as it sounds!" Meagan fired twice more before unleashing a missile. "This should do it."

The pirate veered off from Mick, giving him some relief and tried to escape the missile. Meagan was convinced she'd finished the ship off but at the last second, the pirate dropped something from their ship. Their thrusters flared and the missile exploded, leaving the vessel totally unscathed.

"Did you see that?" Meagan asked. "I mean, seriously…"

"Yes, let's take that one down together."

They started to move in behind it but the ship had disengaged, flying toward the facility. "Hold up," Meagan called. "The mining station is still under control of the pirates. If we get too close they could start firing at us…and honestly, we don't have time."

"There're two more out here somewhere anyway," Mick said.

"Negative," Panther Three said. "We took care of the last two."

"Let him go," Meagan said. "Let's just stay on task and save that ship. Gun it, drop ship. You're clear to target."

***

Olly glanced over his shoulder to report. "Marines are boarding the Alliance ship now, sir. The drop ship has arrived."

"Revente's reporting they got into a pretty harsh tussle with those pirate ships," Adam said. "One of them took a little damage...Panther Four it looks like."

Gray nodded. "Do you have a countdown for when that ship's going to blow?"

Olly turned back to his terminal and sighed. "Less than five minutes, sir."

"Is that enough to turn it around?" Adam asked.

"If they're very quick," Olly nodded, "yes, I believe we can get it done."

Clea concurred. "I'll be on the radio and walk them through it as needed, sir. We'll keep that ship online…and all those people alive."

"Not if they have a brawl to get to the engineering section," Adam said. "Any delay will be fatal."

Redding added in, "surely those maniacs aren't going to sacrifice their lives to lose that ship! Seriously, you'd think they'd be abandoning ship!"

"We can hope," Gray said. "But they set the ship to blow…maybe they're far more zealous than we thought."

"They haven't started killing people on the station," Olly added. "So there must be some kind of disconnect in their ranks."

"Still, they have bombs in the station," Clea said. "That means they're not entirely benevolent."

"I think we need another talk with them," Gray said. "Agatha, hail the station. Maybe they'll consider surrender now that we've boarded them."

"On it, captain."

Gray leaned back in his seat. "It would be nice to find a peaceful resolution to all this...but something tells me we're going to see a lot more bodies hitting the floor before we're done."

***

Hoffner took cover behind a counter for a restaurant on the station promenade. Pirates fired back at them, blasting away without any trigger discipline. They emptied their magazines, wasting dozens of rounds which hammered the walls and buried themselves in the floors. The only thing the criminals got right was warning one another that they were reloading.

The marines dug into good locations throughout different retail outlets, moving into position to finish the conflict quickly. They didn't have an accurate count of the current opposing force but Hoffner estimated less than twenty. His twelve men seemed more than capable of taking down these poorly armed thugs.

Men began reporting in, letting Hoffner know they were in position. They created a wide field of fire, spreading out so they could leverage cover through the entire hallway. Four marines watched their flanks, holding overwatch positions for anyone who tried to come up from behind. Hoffner brought up his HUD and looked at the small cameras on his men's helmets, preparing to give the order.

Each man waited for the moment, poised for action. He listened for the criminals, waiting for one to shout out that he needed to reload. A shrill voice broke, echoing off the wall. That guy would be in cover but his buddies wouldn't be. That was his moment. Hoffner made a two count then called out.

"All units, open fire! Open fire, take them down!"

The marines rose and took precise shots, small three round bursts at the various targets. Hoffner leaned out and took aim himself, shooting into the crowds.

Pirates cried out in pain, their wild fire doing little to provide them any defense. They must've killed a good eight men in the first pass before they dropped back into cover and started a repositioning maneuver.

"I took a hit," one of the marines reported. "Shot to the shoulder. Armor caught the round. Bruising only."

"If it flares up, let us know," Hoffner said. "Otherwise, let's keep up the heat. Don't let these guys get an inch. Call out your drops."

"I've got three confirmed kills," someone said. Another announced two more and still another couple got one each. When Hoffner tallied up the results, he counted nine total. Still quite a few men out there.

Hoffner turned to their local contact, Ander. "Do you know anything about this area that can help us flank these guys? We need to stop playing around."

"Many of these buildings have loading areas," Ander replied. He crouched low, holding his confiscated rifle close to his chest. "They could be used to get around quicker."

"Okay, that makes sense." Hoffner turned his attention back to the battlefield. "I need a volunteer to join me at my position. We're going to flush the game."

"I'm on my way," the man who replied was Camdon, one of his veterans. He didn't join them on the research facility machine but he'd run more missions than most any other soldier on the Behemoth. "Give me a sec."

Hoffner ignored the sounds of gunfire, both the enemy and his men returning it. The marines would allow the pirates to think they had them locked down, unable to move. A little false sense of security would go a long way toward victory. When the marines finally attacked, the shock of it would work to their advantage.

Camdon arrived and took cover across from them behind a downed table. He glanced around the corner and waited for orders. Hoffner gestured to a nearby grocery shop. "That building have the access we need?"

"Yes, sir," Ander replied. "Do you want me to come with you?"

"Negative, stay with these guys. You don't have the armor to risk it." Hoffner patted him on the shoulder. "Thank you for your help so far. We'll be back shortly."

"We going?" Camdon asked.

"Yes, you grumpy bastard. Follow me."

Hoffner dashed out from his cover and moved to the next low table. No one got a chance to take a shot at him before he was out of sight. Camdon took up his rear and they moved into the store, past displays of quick food and nicknacks. The backdoor loomed ahead, a sliding metal affair. A green light on the panel indicated it was unlocked and he tapped the button to open it open.

The second it slid aside, the two marines moved into the loading area, taking a hard left in the direction of their opponents. "We're nearly in position," Hoffner announced. "Standby."

Gunfire continued to echo throughout the area though it was muffled from their position. Hoffner easily differentiated his own men's attacks from those of the pirates. Those fully automatic weapons made a distinct tapping sound when they went off where the marine weapons carried a loud and intimidating explosion with each shot.

There was a finality to when they pulled the trigger and each round sounded loud for the intimidation value. Suppressing them was a bit of a challenge and it tended to require a change in ammunition. Few of the Behemoth's needs involved stealth, especially something like what they were doing on the station and elsewhere, on the Alliance ship.

Hoffner and Camdon reached the end of the loading area and approached a door leading to one of the shops. Camdon hit the panel to open it up and once again, the gunfire blared loud around them, no longer suppressed by the metal walls. They glanced through and found themselves in the perfect flanking position.

Two of the pirates were within view and they didn't even have to exit the alley.

"We're in position," Hoffner announced. "Cease fire and take cover until we give the signal."

A moment later, the marine gunfire ceased. Camdon and Hoffner darted into the room, took cover behind a counter and opened fire. Their rounds riddled the first two men they saw while the others moved. This put them in the open for the other marines. Hoffner motioned for Camdon to drop and they went low.

"Open fire, now!" Hoffner shouted. His men complied, tearing through the enemy forces in seconds. A couple of stragglers started running for it but they didn't make it to the door at the end of the promenade before being taken down. "Cease fire!"

"Want me to start a sweep and clear?" Camdon asked.

"Yeah, grab Aleister. He's good for that." Hoffner checked his com. "Alright, guys. We need access to the control center right away. We've got a bomb to stop so get moving! Ander, you're with us. We're going to need your help access the station's systems. Everyone's got a job people! Move out!"

***

The hangar bay of the Alliance cruiser was abandoned. A couple of alliance fighters sat in various stages of disrepair but no personnel moved about and all the pirate vessels had departed. The marine drop ship put down near the exit and the back ramp dropped down, clanging on the metal deck.

Lieutenant Sander Vincent had been chomping at the bit to command his own mission but this wasn't what he had in mind. Taking a cruiser back from a bunch of pirates with a crazy deadline of you'll die if you mess up seemed a touch excessive. Of course, the parameters changed after his force was committed to the task.

Now to make it happen.

He was the first one off the ship and led his team to the door. Everything had to go perfect or they'd all die. This meant copious help from the Behemoth bridge crew, another part of the assignment he didn't expect. He always assumed he'd work through Lieutenant Colonel Dupont but this time, he needed the help of the Kielan, Clea An'Tufal.

The other team members stacked up on the door, their weapons at the ready. Sander examined the panel and called back to the ship. "We're in position at the hangar door. Can we get some help opening it up?"

"On my mark," Clea said.
"Three...two...one...open."

The door parted in the middle, receding into the walls and his men piled in to clear the hallway. Someone shouted clear and Sander followed them, checking his HUD for the direction they needed to go. The first stop was engineering where they'd prevent the overload from destroying the entire ship. Afterward, they'd free whatever crew members they could find and take back the vessel.

Some of the pirates may still be on board though why, he couldn't imagine. What did they hope to gain by dying there? Denying the prize to the Alliance didn't make much sense. If the criminals just left, they'd live and wouldn't have to sacrifice themselves. Regardless, the more zealous of the people could be anywhere but the marines didn't have the luxury of caution.

"Let's get moving." Sander took point, though in the back of his mind, he knew he shouldn't be. His goal was to show the men he didn't expect anything from them he wouldn't do himself and it had served him well throughout several other missions. Of course, he wasn't the leader then...just an individual contributor.

His team fell in behind him and they hustled down the hallway, practically sprinting. "Contact!" One of the men yelled and gunfire erupted behind them. Sander spun, pressed against the wall and assessed the situation. Two marines opened up, their weapons echoing off the metal ceiling and resounding deep into the ship.

Two people took pot shots at them from an open door where they could pop in and out with perfect cover. Sander's team was out in the open for the most part so they didn't have a lot of option but to shoot back. He pulled a frag grenade and moved to get a better angle. One of the criminals popped out to take another shot.

The weapon fired and slapped one of the marines in the leg, a superficial hit considering the armor but the man probably wouldn't be able to run for a while. Sander cooked the grenade and tossed it so it bounced once just in front of the door and sailed past their two attackers. Two people freaked out inside and one made it into the hallway before the explosion annihilated his buddy.

"Freeze!" Sander aimed his weapon at the guy but one of his men reflex fired and took half the pirate's head off. Sander turned to look at the guy who shrugged.

"Sorry, LT," he said. "You saw how twitchy he was."

"Let's keep our heads cool, gentlemen," Sander announced. "Move out. The clock's ticking."

"An accurate statement," Clea's voice piped into his head speakers. "We're seeing less than five minutes, Lieutenant. I need time to walk you through reversing this so please do hurry."

What do you think we're doing, enjoying the scenery? Sander sighed before replying. "Understood."

They didn't encounter more resistance before reaching the engineering section but it did take them another full minute. As they entered the room, Sander's team cleared the room and he moved over to the primary control console. The entire space looked vastly more high tech than anything on the Behemoth though they were roughly the same in terms of functionality.

Maybe it's the alien aesthetic that gives me that impression.

"I'm in position," Sander said. "Ready to do...whatever you need me to do."

People started shouting clear in various corners and two of his team took up position at the door. Sander bounced on the balls of his feet, adrenaline coursing through his veins. This was intense. They had three minutes before this thing went up. The engines seemed quiet, which was wrong in his opinion. They should be whining at least or building up steam with some kind of grinding sound.

"Alright, I cannot patch into that terminal. It's isolated for a reason. A long time ago—"

"With all due respect," Sander interrupted, "not sure we have time for that."

"Right! So tap the red icon on the left. That'll bring up engine control. I want you to throttle down on the power output. Right now, it seems to be around three hundred percent. You should drop it to ten."

"Why not off?"

"Because we might not be able to reignite the core if you do and these folks need to get that ship home." Clea paused. "I'd hurry. It's picking up the pace. I estimate we have less than two minutes."

Shit! Sander tapped the button and a load screen appeared. Are you kidding me!? If I die because this thing was poorly optimized…

"Have you done it?" Clea asked. "I'm not seeing any change."

"It's freakin' loading!" Sander grumbled. "And it doesn't have a timer…just a percentage. Fifty…sixty…seventy-five…"

"When that finishes, the dial you're looking for is just off the center of the screen to your left. You'll bring it down but again, do not put it to zero. Confirm."

"Yeah, yeah, you're confirmed."

"Contact!" Sander looked over his shoulder to see the door guards firing their weapons.

"How many?" Sander shouted.

"Four!" Davison, the man on the right called back as he fired his gun. "Sorry, three now."

"Keep them at bay!" Sander turned back to the panel. It read ninety-percent. "We're almost there!"

Private Grayson cried out and Sander risked another glance. The young man took a shot to the shoulder and it tossed him to the ground. Another marine took his place as yet a different one pulled Grayson aside to check his wound. The progress bar hit one-hundred percent...stalled...and the screen changed.

"Reducing power now!" Sander reported, sliding it down until he reached ten-percent. "Do what you have to do!"

"You have one more task," Clea's voice remained calm and controlled. Easy for her to be relaxed on the bridge! "I need you to tap in the following access code. Hit the icon on the lower right for a pad."

"Um...these aren't in English!"

"That's okay, I'm going to tell you what to hit by location. Ready?"

"Just go!"

"Upper Right-Lower Left-Middle-Middle-Upper Left-Lower Left."

Sander repeated it back to her despite every nerve ending in his body screaming at him to just do it. She confirmed him when he finished and he slapped in the code. Gunfire behind him made him wince but he focused, willing himself to not turn around. Part of him wanted to ask for a count on the time but he knew he didn't want to know.

"Final code button hit!" Sander said. "What now?"

"Now, I have control of that terminal," Clea replied. "And you're done. Protect the console while I lock down the entire ship to my control only. In a few minutes, you can start releasing any prisoners you might find. Congratulations, Lieutenant. You've successfully saved the Alliance ship."

Thank God for that! Sander turned to his men to assess the situation. "How're we doing? Did you get them?"

"Yes, sir." Davison answered. "Ready for mop up."

"Let's make it happen." Sander tried to sound like his heart wasn't racing in his chest or that adrenaline had nearly made him shake. His command authority remained strong as he stepped out of the room, leading the way to the next objective. He finally felt like he had what it took to be a leader after all.

Chapter 8

Meagan looked at her scanners and had to do a double take. More fighters were incoming, this time from somewhere near the mining facility. They must've been on the actual pirate ship. Readings indicated they were quite a bit better than the ones which tried to prevent the drop ship from docking on the cruiser.

"Giant Control, are you picking this up?"

"Affirmative," Revente's voice came through. "Those are modified alliance fighters. Trying to get a read on what's different."

Meagan performed her own quick scan. The ships were still too far out to engage but they closed rapidly. The computer estimated they'd be in firing distance within three minutes. A few moments passed and the scan showed a holographic image of the incoming vessels. They looked much like the normal alliance fighters only these were heavily armored in the front.

To the point of being excessive. "Why would they have all that reinforced armor?"

Giant Control spoke up, "intelligence suggests that's for ramming tactics. They can do so without compromising their structural integrity. Looks like you've got five incoming."

"To my four. Any chance for some backup?"

"Probably not before they arrive," Giant Control said. "But we'll send them in."

"Can someone get on the cannons and help us out on the cruiser at least? The ramming thing really bothers me."

"I'll see what we can do. Stay alive out there. You're doing great so far."

"That's not as comforting as you might think."

"Hey, I'm an optimist. I'll get back to you soon."

Meagan patched in to the rest of her wing. "You guys see these incoming?"

"Got them on scan," Mick said. "They're better equipped than the last ones."

"But if their pilots are just as bad, it won't matter," Shelly said. "Let's just take care of them so we can go home."

"Don't get too cocky," Meagan warned. "They're setup to ram."

"That's just a crappy tactic," David said. "But you know what, screw them. We've got this."

The computer warned that the ships were nearly in firing distance. Twenty seconds in fact. Meagan ordered her wing to pair off and get ready for a fight. The other ships let loose a torrent of pulse blasts and Panther wing veered off in two separate directions. Meagan saw flashes out of the corner of her eye, more fire from one of the enemies.

"They are all over me here," David shouted. "Wow, they're pretty good too. Let's see if he knows this maneuver."

Meagan altered course, preparing to help David out with some rear support. She got him on visual just as he pulled up then suddenly hit his side thrusters. It was a gutsy move, one that his opponent didn't see coming. The pirate flew right past and David opened up, tearing into the engines and ultimately destroying the fighter.

"Scratch one!" David called out. Meagan opened her mouth to speak and gasped. The pirate may not have meant to sacrifice himself but he gave one of his companions a path, a chance to attack directly after a momentary victory. The ship flew from David's bottom, on a direct collision course.

"David! Pull up!" Meagan shouted, jamming her throttle forward and firing some warning shots. "Now!"

David complied without question but he moved too late. The pirate craft cut directly into his side, tearing a huge chunk out of his fighter as it flew through. "I'm bailing out!" David's com filled with static as he punched out, his pod bolting away from his ship as it exploded in an oval, red blast.

"David!" Mick shouted. "You okay? Can you read me?"

"Focus," Meagan replied, working hard to keep emotion out of her voice. "We'll worry about him when we're not in trouble. Shelly, form up on us and let's play this by the numbers. If we don't stay sharp, they'll do the same thing to us."

"On my way," Shelly said.

Meagan redirected, forming on the tail of the guy who just took David out of the fight. He maneuvered well but there was a distinct lack of discipline. These pilots weren't at all conservative. Every motion they made, every time they course corrected, it was extreme...as if they weren't entirely familiar with the ships.

The targeting computer made lightning quick calculations to catch his motions and locked on in only a few seconds. Meagan pulled the trigger, adjusting slightly to lead him. The first blasts missed and just as he thought to make a dramatic course change, the next three caught him right on the cockpit.

His ship became a fiery ball so fast he couldn't have ejected and Meagan climbed to avoid the debris.

"That's two," she muttered. "Mick, how're you doing."

"Playing tag with these two bastards."

She glanced out to the left and saw them flying in great loops, occasionally taking potshots at one another. Shelly faced off with the last one, spinning her ship in a move that would've killed a pilot if they were in a lesser craft, one with poor dampeners. The pirate nearly rammed her but her top thrusters took her just below him.

Shelly used her thrusters to turn in place and fired while spinning, eyeballing the shots. One clipped the engine of the pirate and the others missed but it was a good blow. It hampered the maneuvering abilities of the fighter and he started back toward the station. "Oh no you don't," Shelly called. "I'm not letting you run after all that."

"If you can't get him fast then don't give chase," Meagan said as she turned to help Mick. He managed to take one of them out while she was paying attention to Shelly but the other one got a good lock on him. Mick tried to juke to the right but two blasts caught him in the side, flaring his shields.

"Whoa!" Mick shouted. "They overloaded my defenses! Crap! What are they firing?"

"Are you okay?" Meagan tried to get in behind the guy but he dove, trying to lead her away. She gave chase. "Mick, report!"

"I'm having my computer shut down my defensive matrix for a second while it recalibrates. Whatever he hit me with was like...I don't know, it tried to make my shield generator explode. Nasty tactic!"

"Not as nasty as this." Meagan fired in front of the pirate and he turned to the right. She did it again, driving him away from the station. Finally, she aimed to the left and dumb fired (leaving the guidance disengaged) one of her last missiles. Then, as it flew from her ship, she took a couple shots at the fighter again, getting him to veer toward her projectile.

He tried to avoid it, firing his countermeasure but it ignored them. He must've thought it was leaving him alone so he started to bank, getting ready to re-engage. That's when she remotely triggered the guidance system. The missile pulled up and connected with the bottom of his ship, knocking the shields out and sending him into a wild spin.

She closed on him, firing with her pulse cannons. Without shields, the ship was torn apart, the core popping a second later.

"One left to go. Shelly? You okay?"

"I've almost got him…" Shelly replied. "Come on, you ass. Just get in my sites already."

"Let him go," Mick said. "He's almost back at the facility."

"Sir, I've almost got him. Five more seconds."

"Make them fast…"

Meagan watched, moving to catch up just in case. Shelly fired a few times but the pirate didn't respond. He was full throttle, trying desperately to escape…or so they thought. Shelly accelerated to catch up and that's when he dropped his power and spun on her, engaging full throttle. They were going to play a game of chicken.

"Don't get in on that!" Meagan shouted. "He won't veer!"

"And I won't have to." Shelly fired three times and banked. Her blasts connected with the nose of the fighter and the shields flared but he didn't go down. Instead, he pulled up after her, trying to catch her engines with his nose. He barely missed, by mere meters if not less. Meagan let out a sigh of relief.

"Stop messing around, Shelly. Get back here."

"He's engaged," Shelly said. "He's not fleeing anymore."

"We're almost there," Mick said. "Lure him back our way and we'll catch him in a crossfire."

"On it."

Meagan watched, feeling helpless as Shelly played a dangerous game of evasion with the enemy fighter. She got a few good firing arcs but the guy managed to dodge them each time. When finally they got in range, he seemed to realize the tables had turned and he was dramatically outnumbered.

He pulled a turn and burn, accelerating fast even without one of his engines fully intact. The three of them closed in on different sides, Shelly in the back, Mick on the right and Meagan pulling in on the left. They all fired and there was nowhere to really go. Several shots littered his back and top, taking him out.

"David, can you read me?" Meagan called out. "Come in."

"I...read you..." The com went back to static. Must be too much damage.

"Giant Control, I need search and rescue to pull in a pod," Meagan replied. "Please respond."

"This is Giant Control, who's down?"

"Panther Three's ship was destroyed but we took out the five." Meagan checked her scan before continuing. "Scope is clear. We are returning to cover the Alliance ship but need backup."

"You'll have it in five. Deploying search and rescue now. Good work."

Yeah, feels great. Lost another ship. This is getting to be an expensive run at some damn pirates.

***

Rathe checked his firearm before slapping Jordan on the shoulder. "We have to get the hell out of here, man. And not through the front door. They're coming."

"Yeah, I know." Jordan grabbed his own gun and they went through the maintenance chute, down a ladder and into a corridor leading away. "I think I know where this goes."

"Great, it better not be a dead end."

"The other option was definitely that. Those marines would've blown us away." Jordan hurried down the hall, hustling into a sprint. "We have to get back to the ship and get the hell out of here. Do you want to find Thantis?"

"Screw that guy," Rathe cursed. "God knows what he was doing down there but it was not helping us out!"

"If he gets out of this, I'm going to take him out." Jordan checked his tablet. "Okay, I've got the layout of this level. If we keep going in this direction, we should get back to our ship. Then we can jump out of this hellhole before the Earth ship catches us."

"We've lost too damn much on this venture," Rathe lamented. "I can't believe it!"

"Hey, if we survive that'll make it okay," Jordan said. "Look on the bright side."

"It's hard to turn a frown upside down on this one...but you're right. Let's just put this place far behind us."

***

The door to the command center was locked. Hoffner turned to Ander. "Can you get us in there? Security clearance or something?"

Ander stepped forward. "I believe so. Allow me."

He tapped on the console, entering a code. It didn't seem to work. "Um..." Ander tried another...and another. The light remained red. "They couldn't have changed it...could they?"

"Problem?" Hoffner asked. "We're in a bit of a hurry."

"Oh! Wait!" Ander shook his head. "Sorry, we changed the overrides recently. I forgot. Here we go."

Ander entered another code and the light went from red to green. "Unlocked!"

"Okay," Hoffner said, gesturing to two of the marines. "You two are on point. Ander opens the door, I'll toss the grenade. When it pops, you two clear the room on one, ready?"

"Ready!" The two shouted, lifting their rifles. Hoffner prepped the grenade and nodded to Ander. The security guard tapped the panel. The door slid to the side. The grenade sailed into the room, bounced off something metallic and popped. A flash brightened the room, the marines called out one then burst inside.

A moment later, they shouted again, this time "clear!"

"Not good," Hoffner said to Ander. "Seems they've abandoned their post."

"Does that mean we've won?" Ander asked. "That we've got the station?"

"Pretty close." Hoffner walked inside, surveying the area. "Lock this place down. I want two men to stay with Ander. The rest of you, we're going to disarm those bombs. You can open the doors down there now, right?"

Ander nodded. "Yes, sir. Let me just get logged in." He moved to a terminal. "I'll have it ready by the time you get down there."

"Okay." Hoffner turned to the men who cleared the room. "You two are with him. Stay sharp. Whoever abandoned this place might come back and if they do, don't mess around. Your rules of engagement stay the same. Shoot to kill."

"Yes, sir!"

Hoffner headed for the door. "Don't disappoint us, Ander. That's not a good place to get stuck in the open down there and God knows how zealous these criminal pricks want to be."

***

Sander Vincent ducked beside an open door as someone fired at them, energy blasts sailing through the door. A pile of metal crates provided some makeshift cover for the criminals. "Stand down!" He shouted. "You bastards don't have anywhere to go so give it up!"

"Don't think they care, LT." One of his sergeants said over the com just as he took a couple shots. "I think they're only getting out of here feet first."

Someone screamed down the hall, a man followed by another person calling out, "retreat! Get to the hangar!"

Wow, these guys… Sander crouched and peered around the corner with his gun leading the way. A pirate made a break for it and was followed by three others. The marines opened fire, putting them down before they made it thirty paces. No drop ship for you.

Sander rushed down the way with two men close behind. They hurried up to the cover and vaulted over, clearing the next room. The three bodies were sprawled on the deck, blood splattered on the walls. Someone pounded on a door just up to the left, shouting for help.

Their cries were muffled but the intent was unmistakable.

"Crew?" Sander turned to one of his men.

"No clue...should we chance it?"

"Who's there?" Sander shouted. "Announce yourself!"

"I am Anthar Un'Cian! I command this vessel! Who are you?"

"Lieutenant Sander Vincent of the USS Behemoth. We've taken this ship back from the pirates. Where's the rest of your crew?"

"They're locked in their quarters all around you! Let us out and we can help take the ship back!"

"I'm pretty sure the pirates have left," Sander replied. He examined the console and noticed they simply locked it from the outside. He clicked it to open it up and two of the marines aimed their weapons in anticipation. As the door slid to the side, a kielan man lifted his hands over his head. His blue-white hair was wild and his clothes were disheveled.

"Please don't shoot!"

"Lower your weapons." Sander waved his hand. "Anthar, you need to get your people back to the bridge and whatever other stations are required."

"What's going on?"

"Your vessel was used to take over a mining facility," Sander replied. "Now there are bombs planted in the place and if we can't get them disarmed...well, they might cause this ship a lot of damage."

"Alright, young man." Un'Cian stepped out into the hallway. "Help me get these doors open and we'll get underway as soon as we can."

"There may be more pirates," Sander replied. "We're going to clear a path for you to the bridge. Follow us when you can."

Un'Cian nodded. "Alright, good hunting and thank you again. I appreciate this more than you know."

Sander contacted the Behemoth. "This is Lieutenant Vincent. We've freed the crew and they'll be heading up to the bridge in a moment to take control. We're clearing a path for them. Expected time to total control, less than ten minutes."

"Very good," Marshall replied. "Keep me informed of any road blocks."

They rounded a corner, weapons lifted. Blaster fire opened up, nearly taking Sander's head off. He dropped to the ground and rolled toward the nearest door. Reaching up, he slapped the panel and moved inside the room. Another marine joined him but the third man lay dead on the ground, his head blackened from the energy blast.

"No! Damn it!" Sander leaned out and opened fire, catching one of the pirates in the face. Blood misted out, spreading over the wall. Another stood, preparing to aim but Sander put one in his chest and one in his face. "Anyone else? Come on out!"

He covered the hallway. "Get him in here." His companion dragged their fallen into the room and checked him out. "Is he…"

"Yes, sir. He's gone."

"Sons of bitches." Sander scowled and stepped out, aiming as he walked. His fellow followed and the others entered the hallway as well. They marched down to the two dead men and checked the area before clearing the elevator. "We need to get up to the bridge but we'll have to use the ladders."

He checked the schematics and popped the maintenance hatch. Their destination was two floors up. He took the lead, climbing up. The others fell in behind him and they hurried up to the second landing. The door opened into a maintenance passage that circled the bridge. Various access points were closed up but the control center of the entire ship was just on the other side.

They stacked up on one of them and Sander did the honors. When they entered, filing in with their weapons and shouts to surrender, they found a lone man with his hands held high. A pirate screaming that he gave up. They discovered that his foot was cuffed to the helm. Sander approached.

"Why'd they leave you here?"

"I told them they were crazy for trying to blow the ship up," he replied. "I don't want to die, guys just…can you please arrest me?"

Sander considered blowing him away for a few moments but finally lowered his gun. "Take this jack ass into custody. The others will be here any moment and we can finally go home." He paused. "Hey, buddy, where's your other ship?"

"I have no idea," the pirate replied. "We got here and they went somewhere near the station."

"Worth a try." Sander went to the communication station and dialed in the Behemoth. "Behemoth, this is Lieutenant Vincent. We have control of the bridge and the crew is on their way."

"I'll release the computer when they arrive," Clea replied. "Excellent work, Lieutenant. Thank you for saving that ship."

"Yeah, no problem, Behemoth." Sander turned and leaned against the console. If he hadn't been wearing the helmet, he would've wiped his brow. Seriously, I think I've set the stage for missions. None of them can be this stressful going forward...

...and I just cursed myself. Good job, Vincent. Good job.

Chapter 9

Olly scanned every bit of the station but the pirate ship somehow eluded him. By the time he finished, he wanted to check his equipment to ensure it was all still working properly. How could they possibly hide such a massive craft? It had to be a freighter. They intended to take Ulem away, enough to make this whole gamble worth it.

He ran a quick diagnostic but it came back fine. A possibility crossed his mind. Maybe they already left. It could've happened after their last communication attempt or even when the Behemoth attacked the Alliance ship. Either way, there were plenty of distractions going on...of course, he was convinced he'd have detected a jump.

Looking back over the logs, he didn't find any unusual energy readings from the facility. No, it was there somewhere but they did a damn good job of hiding it. The Ulem must've masked them somehow. Did they already have a lot on board? He tried searching for a large concentration of the mineral only to feel like an idiot.

It's a mine, there's plenty all over the place.

Olly refused to admit defeat. Now that the Aguna Spear was back under friendly control, he reached out to their tech officer. The man was just getting his bearings but he provided access to their scans. The combined force of both ships might be able to break through whatever interference hid that ship.

The readings came back without good news.

Damn it!

Olly leaned back in his chair and considered the situation. I'm going about this the wrong way. I know! A probe. If I can't find it with scans, maybe a visual search will turn it up. He turned in his seat. "Captain, permission to launch an unmanned probe. I'd like to use it to search for the pirate vessel."

"Can't find it with scans, huh?"

Olly shook his head. "No, I'd like to move to visual search."

"Granted. Let me know what you find."

Olly fired off the probe and took control from his station. The thing proved more maneuverable than he remembered and it took nearly a minute to get the hang of flying one again. He clicked on the recorder and flew it around the facility, starting at the top, circling it then moving downward.

The station was huge and it looked like it would take a while. He set a course with a proximity warning of three hundred meters then turned on the autopilot. Once it finished, he could play back the visuals it sent and use a shape detector to find the ship. Until then, he shifted his focus to checking the area in the event they left.

You have to have left something behind if you rocketed out of here. Everyone makes a mistake. You guys have made plenty.

***

Rathe and Jordan were nearly back to the ship when their com units began to ping. Rathe quickly answered it to kill the sound and crouched, speaking quietly. "Who is this?"

"It's Hannah. You're still alive."

"Which is a lot more than I can say for you when I see you again," Rathe rasped. "You have a lot of nerve contacting us!"

"No choice. Looks like the Earth ship is looking for our freighter."

Rathe sighed. "Of course they are. They won't find it."

"They might," Hannah replied. "They've got a probe out here flying around the station."

"How the hell do you know?"

"I'm in a fighter. Very nearly took out some of their ships too. If I would've had one of the Alliance ships you moved aboard ours, I would've too." Hannah paused. "I'm going to take this thing out and land. I assume you're not back aboard yet?"

"Hannah, I swear to all that's holy in this universe, if you leave without us..."

"I'll just prep for launch, Rathe. Don't worry about it. We'll wait for you guys...as long as we can."

"Hannah!" Rathe slapped the wall when he noticed the communicator was off. "Are you kidding me? Again?"

"She'll leave us," Jordan said. "I guarantee it."

Rathe started to speak but his com went off again. "What am I, a switchboard?" He clicked it on. "Who is this now?"

"Thantis." The voice chilled Rathe's blood. "How're things faring...Captain."

The disdain the man used in the word made both pirates scowl. They stood in silence for a moment before Rathe found a voice to reply. He pursed his lips. "You betrayed us."

"Only a little," Thantis replied. "I did give you more access to the Alliance ship...and helped you control the station, for the most part. My task is nearly complete. There are some marines at the door but they can't undo what I've started. This station, and everyone on board, will be destroyed."

"We're almost to our ship, you sick bastard," Jordan said. "We'll be out of here long before...whatever you're doing...happens." '

"No," Thantis said. "I've ensured your ship is stuck here. I'm sorry, but I really wanted to have some trusted allies with me for this. It's a glorious moment. I'll finally have my revenge and you criminal filth don't get to just waltz in and out like you belong here. History won't know exactly how to label me. Either a criminal or a hero for removing you lot."

Rathe shook his head. "Pretty sure killing hundreds of civilians isn't putting you on anyone's holiday list. You could take out a monster eating people alive in this mess and you'd still be called a fiend. Disarm whatever you've got going on. There's no reason to do this. Whatever your grievance...speaking of which, what could've been so bad?"

"I'm glad someone asked," Thantis replied. "I didn't always limp...nor have these beauty enhancing scars. I worked on this station as a computer expert and got called in for a problem with one of the burrowers. An accident occurred. I'd never been to an unsafe part of the facility before and I...was injured."

"Did you hear the word accident in your story?" Jordan asked. "That means it wasn't anyone's fault!"

"That part was fine. It's the fact that they thought I should retire because I was...no longer fit for duty." Thantis laughed and it didn't sound sane. "They sent me away from my home and friends because of their mistake. I could still function just fine. And what else did I have to do? When I got back to the capital, I couldn't find work. No one would hire the cripple.

"I lived off of government generosity, barely making ends meet. So I saved up...found you...and initiated this plan. No one can fault me wanting my revenge. No one can say I don't deserve to kill them all."

"Um..." Rathe rubbed his eyes. "I'm a criminal and I can say with all certainty, you don't deserve crap. Look, I don't want a bunch of civilians on my conscience for bringing your crazy ass here. You know that if you would've just kept your side of the bargain, we were taking you with us. You could've joined the crew. We need good computer people."

"I don't work for pirate scum."

Jordan laughed. "We're scum? You're about to be a mass murderer! I think you're worse than us, buddy."

"I have a cause!" Thantis shouted.

"Okay, zealot," Rathe said. "Why did you bother to contact us? You've made up your mind. We could've just died here without a clue. Why taunt?"

"I wanted you to know what was about to happen," Thantis replied. "I'll be making a formal announcement to the whole station. That will help these marines keep order...and by that, I mean not at all. People will go into a panic. They'll riot and try to find any means off this station they can but they won't. I've locked down every pod, hangar and escape hatch. You're all here...with me...to the end."

"So you acknowledge this is going to kill you too?" Jordan asked.

"I'd always planned to die here. Good bye, gentlemen. Thank you for the ride."

The line went dead. "How many people are going to hang up on us today?" Rathe shook his head. "He's bluffing. He couldn't have locked down our ship too."

"I'm not so sure," Jordan replied. "I hate to say this, but we might need to help the Earth ship if we hope to get out of this alive."

"No way. We might as well cuff ourselves before we call them."

"It's that or just die."

Rathe considered the alternative for a moment and finally nodded. "Fair point. I'll make the call to the Earth ship...hopefully from ours. And maybe I can smack Hannah around a little bit too. That'd make me feel better."

"You and me both," Jordan replied as they picked up the pace.

***

Agatha received a message from an unknown source. She was about to take it when Olly cursed loudly, drawing her attention away from the console.

"What's wrong?" Captain Atwell asked.

"My probe just got blown up," Olly replied. "Someone actually destroyed it."

"Who?" Commander Everly stepped in. "Do you have a read?"

"Some fighter cruising around causing trouble," Olly said. "Damn pirates."

"Captain," Agatha said, "I've got a com signal from an unknown source. They want to talk to you I think."

"Put them on the screen."

Agatha connected the signal and patched it on the main viewing screen. The pirate who spoke to them earlier appeared on the screen. His face was covered in sweat and he looked tired. Captain Atwell stood up to speak to him. The other bridge staff seemed on edge, as if seeing the man annoyed them.

"Captain," the man said. "So…truce?"

"It's easy to talk about a truce when you're losing," Gray said. "Why are you reaching out to us now? What do you want?"

"So...there were a few things we didn't know about." The pirate cleared his throat and rubbed the back of his neck. "First off, the crazy bastard who set those bombs or...did whatever he's doing...we didn't know he was psychotic. In fact, we just thought he wanted some money. When we got here and he...well...you know..."

"No, I'm afraid I don't. Explain."

"He kind of wants us dead too...for some reason." The pirate frowned. "By the way, my name's Rathe. Good to meet you."

"Uh huh." Gray folded his arms over his chest. "Tell us more about this person. What's their name and why are they doing this?"

"Thantis," Rathe replied. "I have no clue about a surname. He's messed up though, I can tell you that. Got in some kind of accident that screwed up his face and gave him a limp. He's pretty bent out of shape over it too since he plans on killing everyone on this station in retribution. We think that's unnecessary."

"Good to know," Gray muttered. "Clea, take a look at the database for someone named Thantis."

"On it sir."

"So...can we help...at all?" Rathe shrugged. "We're just kind of stuck here until that guy's taken down."

"What do you mean?" Gray asked.

"He somehow fused the docking clamps so we can't manually retract them. We're here until we get access to the computer and frankly, that's not looking easy all things considering. I figure you guys have a chance to make all this right and save the people on board, right?"

"I assume your help comes at a cost."

"It would be nice if we didn't go to prison," Rathe said. "Beyond that, we're pretty open to negotiation."

"Now," Gray finished for him. "You're open to it now. You weren't before. In fact, you even threatened hostages at one point."

"Captain, that was a bluff..."

"And then you attacked us with drones."

"A zealous attendant who was supposed to be watching our cruiser..."

Gray interrupted. "Finally, you tried to blow up the ship, taking the crew and whoever else happened to be close by with it."

"Again, that was the zealot. She started all that trouble with the ship. We were just trying to steal some Ulem. Not nice, but certainly not violent and dangerous. Come on, you can trust me here. We're on your side."

"I'm very curious what exactly you think you bring to the table. From where I'm standing, you don't have much. We've taken the ship back and we just taken the station's command center. I grant that we haven't found your other ship yet but it's just a matter of time. What makes you think you can do anything for us we can't do for ourselves?"

"Look, I know you've got soldiers all over the place on there and you think you've got the entire place locked down...but as you say, you haven't been able to find our ship yet. That means we're pretty crafty. I don't think you're going to locate Thantis and to be honest, I'm pretty sure we're going to need his sneaky ass to clean up his mess."

Adam turned to Agatha. "Ensign, please mute the line."

"Aye, sir." Agatha tapped the control and returned her attention to the captain and first officer.

"We don't need these bastards," Adam said. "They know they've been beaten and they're just hoping that we give them a pass. This is nothing more than a last act of desperation. I say we let Marshall's people take them into custody after they stop the sabotage."

"They're an asset," Gray replied. "I'm not saying they're guaranteed to contribute but consider what's at stake. I'm not saying we just let them go but we've got a lot of civilians over there. If this Thantis person is required to fix whatever he broke, then a criminal to catch a criminal makes sense."

"I respectfully disagree. Making a deal with them will only cause us more trouble than it's worth."

"I'll hear them out. We're just sitting here anyway." Gray turned to Agatha. "Make the mic live, Ensign." She nodded and he picked up the conversation. "Alright, Rathe. Tell me how exactly you can help us."

"Thantis spent a lot of time on our ship while we planned this caper," Rathe replied. "We know him. Tell your guys to stand down while we conduct our search for him."

"Why wouldn't he just be with his work? He plans on destroying the entire station and it doesn't seem like he's trying to escape."

"I promise he's got a plan. The twisted bastard can't enjoy his revenge if he's dead." Rathe shook his head. "How about this, you can't search the entire station. We'll take the lower decks and you guys...keep doing...whatever the hell you're going to do. Keep in contact and we'll catch him."

Gray hummed, turning away. Agatha watched intently, noting the disapproval of Commander Everly. They'd definitely have words later if the Captain allowed the criminals to help. She saw them work together for a long time and they rarely had disagreements but when they did, the tension got pretty thick.

"Okay," Gray turned back to the screen. "You've got a shot. Find Thantis, if you can."

"And...will you let us go?"

"No promises," Gray said. "Besides, we're not the only ones you have to worry about here. The kielans have a big grievance with you and they just got back their battlecruiser back. You'll be lucky if they don't blow you away."

"I guess that's as good as we're going to get." Rathe sighed. "Okay, captain. We'll do what we can and let you know."

The connection dropped and Agatha turned her attention back to her post. She didn't want to see what happened next. Commander Everly and Captain Atwell would likely need a private minute in the office but that wouldn't happen for a while. Clea kept them busy when she spoke up.

"I have Thantis Ga'Vius on file, sir." Clea gestured to the screen and brought a picture up of a tall, thin man with black hair and a severe expression. "He held the highest computer classification for a civilian and worked as one of the chief operators here maintaining the reactor."

"Anything else?" Gray asked.

"Just his service record...exemplary for the most part. A little severe. On his exit report, his coworkers described him as a difficult man who was overly severe and unkind. They weren't really sad to see him go."

"That's messed up," Redding said. "Poor guy."

Timothy shook his head. "That poor guy is about to blow up a lot of people, Stephanie."

"Enough," Gray said. "What else?"

"When he got let go, he dropped off the grid. And..." Clea paused. "Um...he has no family."

"That's bad, isn't it?" Adam asked. "I mean, kielans take that very seriously."

"The Ga'Vius family were having a reunion. There weren't many...seven total. They died in a traffic incident. Thantis missed the event by a day."

"So it wasn't just that he got fired," Gray said. "He lost everyone he cared about in the same month."

"Motive," Adam said. "Can we use this?"

"Maybe." Gray rubbed his chin. "Feed the information to Marshall's people. They might need it if it breaks down to a negotiation. Maybe the Alliance ship can help us but either way, get a report on where they're at anyway. I have a bad feeling we're running out of time."

Chapter 10

Hoffner's marines stood near the door to the reactor chamber. The viewport revealed an abandoned room but there were several devices with flashing lights. If they were the explosives, they'd be busy for a while. He counted at least ten positioned all around the area. The reactor itself was contained, the protective metal plates remained in place.

"Ander, we're in position. Can you get the door open?"

"On it." Something clicked above them, the door thumped and slid into the walls.

The marines rushed in to clear the room, their weapons leading the way. Hoffner paced close to the device on his left and examined it. It didn't look like any bomb he'd seen before and he'd worked with explosives many times. He brought out his scanner and aimed it at the thing for a moment.

There were no explosives in it. In fact, it wasn't a detonator at all. It transmitted some kind of signal but the readings didn't make sense. What did this guy intend to do? He did a quick count: ten in total. He got on the com, patching Ander and Marshall onto the same line. "Gentlemen, I think we've got a real problem."

"What's going on?" Ander asked. "Are you in the room?"

"We're in," Hoffner replied. "But these things aren't bombs. They're transmitters, throwing a signal. I'm sending the readings to the Behemoth now."

Marshall replied, "I'll get Lieutenant Darnell on this now."

"Yeah...there're no timers, no bombs...just these." Hoffner sighed. "No idea what we do with these so we're going to just guard them for now."

"Sounds good," Marshall said. "Stand by."

***

Rathe leaned back after the Behemoth killed the connection. He got what he wanted but would it really do a lot of good? It was better than sitting around doing nothing, at least until his people figured out how to get the docking clamps free. Still, Thantis deserved to pay for what he'd done.

Jordan laughed suddenly. "You're going to love this. Hannah just requested landing clearance."

"Oh, grant it. I'll give her a proper greeting." Rathe drew his weapon and headed down to the hangar. He waited in the hallway until her fighter landed and she hopped out. Before she got twenty feet, he stepped inside and aimed his gun at her head. "Welcome aboard. Glad you could make it."

"Didn't think I'd see you again," Hannah replied. "Put that gun away, we have to get out of here."

"Can't actually. The docking clamps are holding the ship in place and we're kind of screwed." Rathe shrugged. "I just made a deal with the Earth ship. No thanks to you."

"I tried to take them out." Hannah shrugged. "Seriously, quit pointing that weapon at me or you and I are going to go round and round."

"You're a cocky bitch, you know that?" Rathe shook his head "You lost the cruiser, got our fighters torn up and put us in a serious situation with those soldiers out there. Why do you think I won't kill you right now?"

"Because you're running out of crew," Hannah said. "And I'm one of the only pilots you've got left. Hell, I'm probably the only one competent. You think Jordan can get us out of here? You're wrong."

"I'll take my chances."

"So what, you're going to shoot me in cold blood? What deal did you make?"

"I told them I'd find Thantis for them."

Hannah laughed. "Bluffing? That's stupid. You won't find him. Were you just buying time?"

"Or good will. If we don't free the ship, we're going to be captured. What then?"

"I guess we go to jail but I've got a better plan." Hannah grinned. "Put the gun away and hear me out."

"This better be good...hell, I don't even know why I'm listening to you. If I wasn't so desperate...what do you have?"

"Gun?"

Rathe lowered it hesitantly, glaring. "Go."

"Forget Thantis. This place is gone. Screw the alliance and the Earth soldiers. Let them figure this out."

"You're forgetting about the damn docking clamps." Rathe shook his head. "I mean, I appreciate your sentiment but it's a little flawed."

"Easily done. We seal off the hallway to the airlock. Then, we breach both and let the air do the work. Yes, we'll experience some structural damage and it's a little risky but we'll be free to go. Neither the alliance nor the Earth people can chase us because they've got bigger problems. I'll get us out of range and jump to a friendly port."

"With nothing to show for this trip and damage we have to repair." Rathe sighed, rubbing his eyes.

"But…I can't argue with you. It's a better idea than getting arrested but still, I'd hoped to get that Thantis bastard back for screwing us over."

"Revenge is expensive," Hannah said. "He'll get his. Besides, there's always another score. If you don't remember that, then you've forgotten what it is to be a pirate."

Rathe paced, unsure exactly whether he wanted to trust her. He wanted to slap the crap out of her still but she made too many good points. She'd always been a pain in the ass and this situation was no different. None of her antics cost them so dearly in the past. Their losses this time numbered too high to count.

If they betrayed the Earth ship, they'd need to keep their head downs for a long time. Every benevolent government would be after them. Plenty of places could harbor them until the heat died down. Until then, they'd have to live off what meager savings they had. At least we don't have to share as much now…morbid ass thought considering how many people we lost.

"Alright, Hannah. You're on. Let's get out of here...if we can."

"Oh we can," Hannah said, pacing past him. "If there's one thing I've always been it's a survivor. Just follow me and I'll show you how."

***

Olly got the readings from Marshall and looked them over, his eyes wide. He'd seen a lot and studied all sorts of technology, both in school and out. These devices baffled him. They sent a signal out into the station but he didn't see the point. What were they communicating with? Nothing replied back. Their broadcasts were one way.

Are they talking to a bomb? A highly complex detonation device? It seems so...unnecessarily convoluted. I mean, an explosive device just has to go boom. Was he so convinced that someone would come along and disarm his work? Maybe so...Maybe it's worse than we know.

Olly brought up the schematics for the station and skimmed down to how it maintained position around the planetoid. Mining operations took place down below, deep in mine shafts which laced into the ground. Asteroids connected to the facility were also mined though to a much smaller extent.

Orbit was maintained with massive thrusters powered by the pulse reactor where the weird devices were located. Course corrections were made in the control room, not by pilots but trained computer technicians who were qualified to check the automated calculations. Thantis had been one such person to hold that responsibility.

Maybe they're talking to the computer somehow. Wait!

Olly pulled the signal into his computer and ran it through the universal code. It translated it far slower than he anticipated and it shocked him. He had yet to encounter anything complex enough to give that code a problem. Now, as it displayed the intention of the signal, he realized Thantis had designed this from the ground up to communicate with the devices he was most familiar with.

The computers of the station had been under his control for a long time. He knew them better than anyone probably. So this signal was talking to the station, making minor course corrections so that any failsafe would not be triggered. Olly checked the logical progression of what he intended and sunk in his seat.

Thantis intended to have the station crash into the planetoid. Not only would it destroy the station but the Ulem source as well. It wouldn't cripple the alliance but the loss would certainly be felt. Economically, they'd get hit but the military programs relying on the mineral would especially feel the pain.

The navigation computer used to interface with the thrusters was locked down, secure from manual or remote access. Thantis had changed all the passwords and erected a special firewall. It felt a bit like what he'd done to the Alliance ship but Clea got through that. Unfortunately, she probably wouldn't know this system as well as the military ones and he didn't know it either.

Olly calculated out how long before the facility crashed. Maybe they had enough time to do some trial and error. He gasped. Holy crap! Are you kidding me? He stood up. "Um...captain, we have a serious problem."

"Explain."

"Those devices are interfacing with the computer and slowly taking the facility into the planetoid. This guy locked everything down and it's practically his proprietary system. While I'm not saying it's unhackable, I'm saying it's pretty damn close...but even if we could, we only have about ten minutes before it happens."

"Ten minutes? Are you sure?"

Olly nodded. "Yes, sir. This thing is going down and it seems like the only way we're going to stop it is to catch the person responsible and make them give us their codes."

Gray turned to Adam. "Tell Hoffner now. They need to get that guy." He turned to Clea. "Get with Olly and look into this computer code. Find out what you can do and if you can get through this guy's security. Let's move, everyone. Once again, we don't have time for mistakes so let's keep things tight and by the numbers."

You're telling me. Olly thought as he sent the information over to Clea's tablet. Let's hope she has more ingenuity than me. Man, I'd love for one mission to not be a serious of time limits intersecting. That'd be swell.

***

Gray leaned back in his seat and forced himself to relax, ignoring the threat of a headache building behind his eyes. The part of their mission he thought would be the most difficult, they'd managed but taking back the facility now proved the more challenging. He believed they'd take it back with relative ease but now, everyone on board was at risk.

"Adam, we should evacuate the station just in case," Gray said. "Let's get shuttles moving now."

"Sir, we can't get all those people off there in ten minutes," Adam said. "And the pirates locked down all the escape pods."

"We have another problem," Timothy said. "It looks like our pirate friends have decided they don't really want to help us."

"What do you mean?" Gray asked. "What did you find?"

"Just an energy build up and some motion on the scanners." Timothy took a moment to dial something in. "Yes, I think they're trying to break free of the docking clamps."

"Are they insane?" Adam asked. "They'll kill themselves!"

"If we're lucky, they'll be the only ones," Timothy said. "There are only a few things they could even try and none of them are particularly safe. Speeding off with their engines might work—they could tear the wall out with them but I'm thinking they might be trying to blow the airlock."

"Why do you say that?" Adam asked.

"Because there's a safety beacon going off in that section stating one of the seals is giving out. I doubt that we're seeing wear and tear settling in right now."

"That would be just perfect," Gray muttered. "These guys...first they want to help then they turn tail and run?"

Adam shrugged. "They're criminals. I'm not sure what you expected of them."

"I don't know...some more integrity I guess." Gray sighed. "Okay, so we can't rely on them...not that they were going to be much help anyway. Let's just focus on the task at hand. Clea, do you have anything?"

"No, sir." Clea replied. "The security this man installed is frankly genius. It's elegant and simple, making it difficult to interface with. Worse, he's cut it off from the other computers on board so we can't even get any help. I have little confidence in taking him into custody either."

"Why?" Adam asked.

"Because if he's zealous enough to kill all these people, I doubt he'll break in the short time we have to get the information from him."

"What about detaching the devices?" Gray asked. "Or destroying them?"

"The metal casing he used is pretty tough," Olly said. "And worse than that, we don't know how many there are. From what I can tell, they're all broadcasting the same signal. They're probably all failsafes...oh, and I have worse news."

"You're just a bundle of joy, Oliver," Adam grumbled.

"I know...but...anyway, he tampered with the reactor. When that thing hits the ground, it'll blow...and think about this. We've used alliance reactors to blow up enemy vessels. That thing is five times as big. It'll be catastrophic."

"Great...Okay, let's hope he's got a switch on him or something." Gray tapped his communicator and patched in to Hoffner. "Listen up, Captain. I don't want to put too much pressure on you but you have to find this guy now or everyone on that station and probably us too will be dead."

"Yeah, we kind of figured," Hoffner replied. "We're on it, sir. I'll report back soon."

***

Jordan's eyes nearly bulged from his head when Rathe and Hannah entered the bridge. The fact that the woman was still alive shocked him but when she moved over to the helm and took control, he thought he had to be hallucinating. Grabbing Rathe, he dragged him aside and spoke in a hushed tone.

"What the hell is going on?"

"She had a great idea," Rathe whispered back. "I had to take her up on it."

"So let me get this straight: you're completely insane, right? This lady has caused us no end of grief, man! What could she have possibly told you that makes this okay? Seriously, it better be good or I might consider a mutiny."

"Relax!" Rathe lifted his hands to placate him. "Look, she's got a plan to get us out of here and considering what she's managed to survive already, I think we need to take her up on the offer."

Jordan watched as Hannah tapped into the computer, her fingers flying over the touch screen. She leaned to the navigation station and did some work there as well then walked over to the engineering console. There, she pulled some manual release which Jordan had never seen before. Somewhere in the ship, they heard a loud boom.

"Um…" Jordan looked at Rathe. "What the hell was that?"

"She's blowing the airlock where we're docked," Rathe said. "To get us out of here."

"That will kill us!"

"No," Hannah replied. "I sealed off that corridor. Yeah, we won't be able to go down there until we dry dock and repair but combine that with a little thrust and we'll be out of here in no time."

"Some of our men are still on the station!" Jordan cried. "We should at least give them some time to get back!"

"You can join them," Hannah said, "but we're not waiting for anyone. If we don't go now, the Earth ship or the Alliance cruiser will block us in. We have to go. Now."

"That's messed up." Jordan shook his head. "I do not agree with this."

"The good news is you can be indignant and free," Hannah said, "instead of in prison. You can complain at me all you like then."

Hannah took the helm again and ignited the maneuvering thrusters. An alarm went off and the computer issued a warning that the docking clamps were still engaged. The ship began to shake and Jordan took his seat and put on his safety belt. Part of him felt compelled to pray. He didn't feel confident they'd survive this ploy.

"Okay, I'm ready to initiate the blast," Hannah said. "Everyone better hold on tight."

"Blast?" Rathe sat beside Jordan and belted in. "What do you mean?"

"I've pumped an excessive amount of oxygen into that corridor then sealed it up. I've also disengaged every safety protocol installed in the airlock. When I pop them both, the force plus our thrust should break us free."

"Free from this mortal coil," Jordan muttered. Still, he couldn't argue that Hannah was resourceful, even cunning. The risks she was willing to take made him nervous though. Plus, she easily abandoned a bunch of their colleagues and shipmates. He knew full well that if he and Rathe hadn't made it back before her, she'd be leaving them there too.

He always considered her to be a talented person but he never knew just how little regard she held for any of them. When she came aboard, her credentials were staggering and Rathe expressed concern about someone so good being available...or a criminal for that matter. Now, Jordan understood. She didn't get along with people and when her true colors showed, they were not pleasant.

"Five seconds," Hannah said. She glanced back at them with a smile. "Here's where we separate the boys from the women. If you've got prayers, say 'em. Cause this is going to be one hell of a ride."

Jordan complied, praying to whatever higher power he could think of to let him live. Of course, considering the things he'd done with his life, he doubted anyone would listen. Trying gave him a little peace but only superficially. Deep down he knew he'd been a terrible person and whatever happened, he likely deserved.

Then again, people like Hannah had incredible luck. He might be able to take advantage of it and survive this ordeal. Hope tickled his heart as the last couple seconds ticked away. Hannah hit a button. The entire ship trembled and shook as something exploded down below. Jordan yelped just as the ship began to drift away from the station.

"She did it!" Rathe yelled. "Holy crap, good job!"

"We're not out of this yet," Hannah said. "Setting a course away from this place. Engaging thrusters…"

They began to move, powering away from the facility. Jordan wondered fleetingly about the damage done to the station. Would it impact the people left behind? The civilians? It didn't matter. Whatever Thantis had in mind for them would be fatal anyway. Maybe breaching the hull would grant them a swifter death.

He took a quick tally of how many people were on board the ship. Seven pirates were spread throughout the vessel. Seven out of so many. Their crew had been totally decimated. Acquiring another one would take months if not longer but Hannah's message came back to him loud and clear.

At least you're alive and free. Jordan could work with that. Prison didn't sound good and those marines weren't taking any crap. Fleeing, despite how it felt leaving behind his crew mates, was the only real option. I'll find a way to live with it but sorry boys. You'd have done the same.

He spent the next several minutes trying to convince himself that was true.

Chapter 11

Olly focused intently on the signal of the sabotage, working closely with Clea to find a way to reverse it. Something was missing from their part of the puzzle, a key or legend which would express how the computer took the information and processed it. They made some guesses but none of them mattered since they couldn't take control.

The tech officer from the Aguna Spear wasn't much help. He didn't understand the computer techniques as well as Clea so they let him get back to his duties pretty fast. Olly's mind started to wander to alternatives, ideas which might stop the station from moving but none of them seemed plausible.

Disengaging the thrusters through force might work for a time, but it might only delay the inevitable. Of course, they might be able to evacuate the people then. It's thrusters were simply too powerful to counter, even if both the Aguna Spear and Behemoth tried to tow it at the same time.

Clea hummed beside him, eyes narrow as she read something on the screen. Olly understood quite a bit of kielan but whatever the text was on the screen, he couldn't make it out. He turned his attention to another bit of his work. He wanted to penetrate the shielding around one of the devices, hoping that a glimpse of the inner workings would get them further along.

Part of him felt like Captain Hoffner was wasting his time looking for Thantis. What would he possibly have to say? If he was so crazy as to want to kill all those people, he wouldn't just fold under a little pressure. And they didn't have time for much. Maybe if he had a device with the last piece of the puzzle, the code to control the various signal emitters…but if not, they were done.

"I've analyzed the signal," Clea said. "I'm afraid you were right about missing a piece. We can emulate what it's saying but it's so singular, so simple that there's no room for interpretation. Technically, there's no reversal either. All these are doing are reinforcing the course corrections but from what I've gathered, they're sequentially programmed in. Even if all those devices were jettisoned, it would get to the end eventually."

"I don't know what's inside them either," Olly said. "For all we know, if we tried to remove them, they'd blow up…or worse, start a different signal to another computer. That's all we need."

"So far, we're under the impression that all the devices are transmitting the exact same signal," Clea said. "Can we put them on the screen and compare them? Side by side, maybe there's some discrepancy we can exploit."

"I've checked a couple of them," Olly replied, then paused. "Wait a moment…"

"What? What've you thought of?"

"The signals are all the same but are they going at the same time?"

"I don't follow you."

Olly brought all the devices up on his scanner, showing their signals. "Watch as they begin to transmit."

Each one started at a different time, emitting its message for half a second before the next began. They found there were thirty-two total devices, all going at different times. He smiled. Now we're getting somewhere!

Clea narrowed her eyes. "You think that while the signals all appear the same, together they're transmitting a complete set of instructions, is that it?"

Olly nodded. "Timing is the key, not specifically what they're currently saying. As they ping the computer, it essentially is checking boxes. I think I've got the first one so I'm going to compile the entire message and see if we're still missing anything."

"Excellent work, Lieutenant but we need to hurry."

"Oh, I feel it." Olly nodded. "Here we go."

***

Timothy was watching the scans while Olly occupied himself with the bigger problem. His eyes widened as he caught a large ship departing the station at a rapid clip. He zeroed in and did a check against the database. It was a large, modified freighter...the pirate ship finally revealed itself and it had indeed been responsible for the broken seal.

"Sir, the pirates are leaving the station," Timothy said. "They managed to tear themselves free after all."

"They're getting away?" Adam frowned. "We don't really have the time to pursue them."

"Sir," Agatha announced. "I have the Aguna Spear on com. They're saying they can pursue the pirates and take care of them."

Gray nodded. "They have a score to settle so let them do it. Tell them to keep us informed of their progress but I'm pretty sure those criminals are heading for a minimum safe distance to jump."

"Looks like it," Timothy said. "I'm tracking their course and they're putting as much stuff between us and them as they can. I estimate they'll make it to their destination in less than three minutes at current speed."

"We also know they don't care about safety," Adam said. "They just ripped free of docking clamps after all."

"Warn the Aguna Spear." Gray scowled. "The fact that they had their ship taken makes me want to give them any advantage we might be able to afford."

"On it, sir." Agatha paused. "They say they're on a pursuit course and will report back soon."

***

Hoffner sent the other marines to sweep and clear to eliminate or capture the remaining pirates. When the entire station began to shake, he leaned against the wall. An alarm went off overhead and a computer shouted something about a hull breach and how it was initiating a containment field.

He patched his com into the control center. "Ander, what the hell just happened?"

"I think the pirates just yanked themselves free of the station," Ander replied. "They destroyed a wall in the process! Wow...they didn't want to say."

"I guess I can't blame them," Hoffner said. "I need your help. We have to track this Thantis guy down. My men are looking for pirates. You and I need to get him. I'm relying on you to know this place better than me. Where would he go? Do you think he's trying to kill himself?"

"Hm...all shuttles and escape pods are locked down...wait!" Ander grunted. "One of the hangars...someone just broke a seal down there. He must be in there!"

"I'll meet you in the promenade." Hoffner began to run. "Catch up to me there and lead me to this place. We'll take care of him together."

"What's the plan?"

"Interrogation...and hopefully, negotiation. Hurry."

Marine chatter over his com indicated they located additional enemy forces. Most of them surrendered. The few who had any fight in them took some shots but they were quickly overwhelmed. When he arrived at the promenade, Ander hustled up to him and pointed down the hallway. They moved off together at a steady run.

Ander tapped Hoffner on the shoulder and slowed down, gesturing to a large set of doors just ahead of them. They were easily big enough to bring in heavy cargo, the types of lifters and burrowers they used deep in the mine shaft. Perhaps freighters docked there as well to load up Ulem for transport.

"This is it." Ander tapped at the console and the door started to open. "Oops! I didn't mean to open it right away!"

"We don't have time for subtlety so don't worry about it." Hoffner raised his weapon and stepped inside. There were a few shuttles scattered about but the one in the center took his attention. Their man stood beneath it, performing a preflight check. He didn't seem to notice them, which seemed odd. The doors weren't exactly quiet. "Hey there!"

Thantis turned to them, stumbling back in shock. "How? How did you find me?"

"You broke in here," Ander said, pointing his own gun at the man. "I caught it on the security scans."

"You're the one who warned the Earth ship, aren't you?"

Ander nodded. "I am. I only wish I would've caught you sooner before you sabotaged the station."

Thantis shrugged. "You didn't. Now you get to die here...and me too if you don't let me go."

"You say that like there's a remote possibility I'll let you go," Hoffner said. "I'm going to tell you this just once. If you help us, you live. Otherwise, I'm taking your head off. Sure, other people might die, but you are guaranteed to go down."

"Is your human bravado supposed to scare me?" Thantis spat. "Because if so, I'm not impressed. You don't think I came here prepared to die?"

"No, I don't." Hoffner shook his head. "If you were, you wouldn't be trying to get out of here. You'd sit here and enjoy a front row seat to the mass murder you're about to commit. So let's cut the crap and get to the point. I know you can stop this insanity so let's get to it."

"Do you have any idea what these people did to me?" Thantis shouted, his eyes blazing with rage. "How they humiliated me? Then, I returned to a dead family, killed by the carelessness of my own people! This is the very least I can do to repay them for all that they've done to me. Hit them where it will hurt. In the financials."

"Do any of the people on this station deserve to go through what you did?" Ander asked. "The civilians? How about Tierna? I know she sold you drinks all the time. She didn't have anything to do with you being let go or your family dying yet you're going to kill her! She has family too and you're going to make them suffer."

"Everyone should suffer the way I did."

"Yes, it's all very tragic." Hoffner took a step forward. "Tell us the secret of how you're taking this place down. Let us help you. Lord knows the kielan way of rehabilitating criminals is different from ours. From my understanding, they'll get you some help."

"Forget it." Thantis turned away and continued his preflight check. "I won't help you. You'll just have to shoot me."

Ander put his hand on Hoffner's arm. "Wait! Let me...let me try one more time."

"Hurry." Hoffner said. "We're dramatically short on time here."

"Thantis, please..." Ander advanced on him. "You can't pretend you don't care about anyone at all. What you've been through, I agree, it's awful. I came here because I was tired of the killing, tired of the war but I didn't take it out on civilians. I helped them. You can do the same. Just...join me and the Captain. Put a stop to this plan and I'll be sure you get treatment."

Thantis paused, glaring at the security guard. Hoffner thought, for a brief moment, that the man may actually come around. He seemed to falter in his convictions, if only for a moment. Unfortunately, it didn't last and the crazed expression conquered the placid one quickly. Luckily, Ander kept his gun poised or Hoffner figured Thantis would've tackled him.

"Enough of this!" Thantis cried. "I will not be swayed by your sentimentality. I have fostered this revenge for long enough. None of you can stop me. It's over! For you and these people!"

"He won't break," Hoffner said. "This is your last warning, Thantis. If I have to let these people die, you don't get to be around to enjoy it. Tell us what we want to know or I fire."

"I'll make it easy for you, human scum!" Thantis reached into his jacket and Hoffner pulled the trigger, popping a single shot that connected with his target's forehead. Thantis's eyes widened in shock and he died long before he hit the ground.

Ander rushed to the body and searched his pockets. "He was going for his tablet. Here it is."

"Is it doing anything?"

Ander admired it for a moment and nodded. "Yes, it's definitely working on something. Like...like an application is running but I have no idea what any of this means."

"Behemoth, come in. This is Hoffner."

Agatha answered. "We read you, Captain. Report."

"We've had to kill the terrorist but we have his computer. It's running an application of some sort. Can you tie in to us and get what you need off of it?"

"Patching you through to Lieutenant Darnell."

A moment later, Olly came on. "What've you got?"

"The terrorist's tablet. It's running some kind of application. Can you get to it from there?"

"Maybe. Um...have yours scan it and I'll do what I can remotely."

Hoffner set them down on a nearby crate, side by side. "Okay, do your magic."

He watched as his own tablet was remotely controlled from the Behemoth and a few moments later, it began a scan he didn't know it was capable of. He turned to Ander while he waited. "Did you find anything else?"

"Personal items," Ander replied. "An image of his family...identification...nothing of consequence."

"You sure? Keep looking."

"I'll let you know..."

Hoffner paced, a sense of urgency biting into his gut. They were so short on time but he couldn't really hurry the bridge crew of the Behemoth. If anyone could solve it, their tech officer would find a way...but would he manage to pull it off before it was too late? The few moments they had left would tell.

***

"Clea, check this out!" Olly gestured wildly. "First, I was right. They're working in tandem to send several messages...like...each one is essentially changing the numbers in a binary code. Until right now, I couldn't have told you what they were altering but now, we have the guy's tablet and the key is here! I know the sequence it's using and what it said."

"Can we reverse it?" Clea asked. "What do you have to do?"

"Now that we have the key, I can alter the course of the station, get it back on track. Timothy, can you plot the course for me? Show me what I should have it at?"

"One second." Timothy tapped away at his console and nodded. "You ready?"

"Send them over, I don't want to make a mistake."

"Incoming."

Olly received the new coordinates and frowned. They were dramatically different than the end result of where Thantis wanted the station. He took a quick moment to run a test, to see if his new signal would do what he wanted. The computer suggested it would but he needed someone to manually enter the information.

"Okay, Hoffner, I need you to enter this code I'm sending over. It will alter the course of the station but...you're going to get pretty damn close to the planetoid before it's fully corrected."

"Sounds like a fun ride," Hoffner muttered. "Just get it over here."

Olly sent the information and sat on the edge of his seat, tapping his foot nervously. If Timothy was wrong or Olly somehow screwed up sending the information, a lot of people would be dead. The tension weighed on his shoulders and made his hands shake. They'd been through a lot of crazy situations but this one, with so many civilians at stake, really bothered him.

"Keep us informed," Olly said, turning an anxious look to Clea. She nodded once which he assumed was a kielan way of offering him some comfort. It didn't work but he took a deep breath, crossed his fingers and hoped.

***

Hoffner looked at the information and frowned. *Really, Oliver? That's...not a simple five digit number.*

The readout he received was a long line of code, probably thirty characters. And I've probably only got one shot to get it right. Seriously, why couldn't this guy just have planted a freakin' bomb?

"Are you sure about those?" Ander asked. The station shook, a clear indication that orbit was decaying quickly. It might not stop the next time it started. Hoffner shrugged at Ander.

"I don't think we have a choice. Here we go."

He began to pound the digits in, one at a time, verifying each. There wasn't time for much caution but screwing up would be just as bad as not finishing. The first ten went quick but then he started to get nervous. His mind made him second guess and teased him about failure. As many missions as he'd run, he never felt quite so much weight as putting in a bunch of characters in a tablet.

The last five came and he held his breath. Ander went tense beside him. The station began to rumble. Screams sounded in the hallway beyond the hangar. He knew people were panicking, probably looking out viewports or looking at scanners to see what was happening. They all knew what was at stake but they didn't realize a single man might well save their lives...or condemn them completely.

He finished the last character and hit commit, stepping backward to watch the results. An alarm went off but he had no idea what it was calling out specifically. Proximity? A dramatic course change? It didn't matter, the damn thing started blaring just as the new code went into effect.

Likely, the modified signal needed to force the station to dramatically correct course and that probably set the computer off. That's why Thantis made it gradual, because the computer wouldn't bother with it until the situation was too late. Olly didn't care if the people had to deal with a little siren for a few minutes if it meant saving their lives.

At least, that's what Hoffner believed. The station rumbled again, this time shaking so badly they almost lost their footing. Hoffner grabbed Ander and steadied him and they grabbed the tablets to move closer to the walls. There, they leaned and kept themselves aloft all while the station did a dance around the planetoid.

"Is it working?" Hoffner called into his com. "Behemoth, are we correcting course?"

"Yes!" Olly's voice came through, a shout of excitement. "Yes, we did it! Good work, Captain! We're good! The station's coming back to a regular course and speed!"

Hoffner slumped and turned to Ander. The two men smiled as a sense of relaxation came over them. The station, and everyone on board was safe. Thantis's crazy plan failed and now, they could get back to business as usual. After countless missions, Hoffner could definitely say this was the one that left him with the most relief and definitely thankful for his backup on the Behemoth.

***

Rathe took the scanners and cursed. "Hannah, our alliance ship is following us."

"Okay," Hannah said. "They won't catch up in time. We're about to jump."

"You'd better make it damn fast!" Jordan shouted. "Because they're liable to shoot first and ask questions later."

"They want us alive," Hannah replied. "Because if they kill us, they can't save face for being commandeered. Besides, prisoners are worth more than bodies. Don't worry, they'll go for disabling shots long before—"

A pulse blast nearly hit them dead on but grazed their shields. The ship was jostled and Rathe barely kept from falling over. He turned and glared at the pilot, seething that he'd gone along with her plan.

"You were saying? That felt pretty damn close to an full on attack!"

"Relax, will you?" Hannah shook her head. "They're just trying to scare us."

"Now they're hailing us," Jordan said. Rathe looked at his friend as the man listened to the com. "They're basically telling us to surrender or they'll blow us out of the sky. I think you've bluffed enough, Hannah! Can you please stop putting all our lives at risk because you don't want to go to jail?"

"What do you propose? That we give up?"

Rathe and Jordan replied together, "Yes!"

"Well, I won't do it." Hannah hit the throttle and the ship rocketed forward. Rathe had had enough. He left his station and grabbed her from behind, roughly throwing her from the seat. She hit the deck and rolled, slamming into the wall. He took her seat and slowed them down.

"Jordan, get a gun on her!"

Jordan aimed his weapon as Hannah took her feet. Rathe killed the engines and connected to the Alliance ship, signaling their surrender. Once they messaged back that they would bring them aboard, he turned to his former pilot and shook his head. She sure as hell didn't give up, he had to give her that.

"There's a point when you can't win anymore," Rathe said. "That's when you have to be smart or you'll just be dead. Remember this: no second chances if you're a corpse."

"You think you'll ever get out of prison, Rathe?" Hannah asked. "Because you won't. I swear to you, none of us will see the light of day again."

"We'll see about that," Jordan added. "This way we have a chance to get out someday. Right now...well, you nearly got us all killed. I think you're ready for a time out, girl."

"You should at least let me get out of here with my fighter. I can elude them."

"I don't know why you're so set on this, but no, I'm not letting you. If you jeopardize our chance to live through this, I can't let you do it." Rathe shrugged. "Relax. We'll have our chance...another day in the sun but now, we have to acknowledge defeat."

"You craven bastards deserve what you get." Hannah leaned against the wall. "I can't believe you. We could've gotten away. You should've let me try."

"We did…and now, we're done." Rathe paused as their ship began to shake. The Alliance ship was pulling them. "This is it, guys. It was a good run. Thanks for everything you did. You were all pretty amazing. If I hadn't trusted Thantis, none of this would've happened…but sometimes, the big scores require big risks."

"It's okay," Jordan said. "We'll have another chance…someday."

Rathe nodded. "Someday. Until then…see you after the trial."

***

Chapter 12

Gray leaned forward, waiting for reports to come in. There were a lot of moving parts but the essential ones were Hoffner's attempt to stop the station from exploding and the Aguna Spear capturing the last of the pirates. Olly worked closely with the marine captain to get his job done but things still looked dicey.

They watched the station drawing closer to the planetoid and Gray could cut the tension on the bridge with a butter knife. No one was immune, not Redding or Timothy, Adam or Agatha. Clea and Olly were too intent on their task to show it, but he recognized the signs of anxiety. He knew how much it weighed on the young technician to know his work protected countless lives.

"Report coming in from Hoffner," Olly said. "He's entered the code...Timothy, is it working? The thrusters kicked on and it's trying to correct but...do you have it?"

Timothy did some calculations and Gray waited, practically holding his breath. It took him too long, even as they only seemed to wait for about thirty seconds. Finally, he nodded emphatically. "Yes, it's going to be close but it's working! They should be back to their regular course in less than half an hour but it'll be a bumpy ride for the next ten minutes or so."

"Send a broadcast to the station letting everyone know to stay safe," Gray said. "Agatha, can you tap into their com system?"

"I'm on it, sir."

"How're the pirates?"

"Aguna Spear just took a shot at them," Redding said. "They picked up speed…no! Wait, they're slowing down! Ha! Must've had second thoughts there."

"The Aguna Spear is hailing us, sir," Agatha said.

"Patch it to me."

"This is Anthar Un'Cian of the Aguna Spear. I understand I have you to thank for returning our vessel to us."

Gray nodded. "Indeed, welcome back to command. How long have you been under control of the pirates?"

"Not quite a month," Un'Cian said. "But we're in control now. We've taken a few pirates into custody which were still aboard and now the others who fled in their ship are ours as well. Your men would like to return to you and will be departing shortly."

"Thank you very much."

"No, thank you. We owe you a debt we can never repay."

"I'm just glad you're all okay." Gray grinned. "Will you be able to assist with the station here? Once we've got our people back and everything's stable, we'd like to return home with a consignment of Ulem. We've come a long way to finish up an important project."

"Absolutely. We'll also report in this way and make sure our collective superiors understand what happened here. You're all heroes and I certainly intend to have the record reflect your actions. If there's anything you ever need from me, now or in the future, do not hesitate to ask. I will be sure to help."

"Thank you. I'll let you go as we start to coordinate our people getting back aboard. Let us know if anything comes up." Gray turned to Olly. "I think we should have those devices brought back here for study, don't you?"

"Yes, sir. I've asked Captain Hoffman to grab them before he leaves."

"Good. Let's see, we've saved the station, preserved the Aguna Spear, stopped the pirates and freed all the hostages. I wish I could say it felt easy but good job, everyone." Gray hesitated. "Hey, let's get that security guard on the line. Ander? I'd like to say something specifically to him."

"He's with Captain Hoffner," Olly said. "I've got them on the line now. Patching them over to Agatha for visual."

Ander appeared on the screen with Hoffner, looking exhausted and worn. Still, he managed to smile while he looked down at the tablet and stood up straight as if moving to attention. He didn't look like Gray envisioned. He'd thought the guy would be muscular, a brick of a man but instead, he looked like anyone else.

A soldier perhaps, but a normal person first.

"Hello." Ander waved uneasily. "Thank you for coming to our aid, Captain. Trust me, everyone on board here appreciates it."

"We're glad to have helped," Gray said. "I'm hoping we can link up and take a consignment of Ulem with us. I believe we had an order in for some to finish up a ship but that's not your problem. We'll work with the administrators on that. I just wanted to take a moment to commend your bravery and ingenuity. Your intel was invaluable and I know it couldn't have been easy."

"No, it sure wasn't…but thank you. I appreciate the compliment."

"I hope we might meet in person before we leave this sector but for now, I'm sure you men have things you'd rather be doing. We'll talk again. Hoffner?"

"Yes, sir?"

"Great work. I believe you men are helping with clean up and security, correct?"

"Just until the local security force is back in control," Hoffner replied. "Then we'll be taking the drop ship home. Shouldn't be too long. I'd give it six hours before we've managed any unrest and answered questions. May I recommend we bring over some medical crews? I suspect we'll need some supplemental help."

"Good thinking. We'll organize something right away. Let us know if you need anything else. Gray out." He turned to the others. "Alright, ladies and gentlemen, let's coordinate our efforts. We've got some search and rescue to conduct, salvage, some station work and medical aid to send. Reports to my station. I'd like to have a positive report to send inside of the next two shifts. Let's go."

***

Ander helped the marines free the hostages from their homes, unsealing door after door. The people's gratitude overwhelmed him with emotion and by the time he freed Tierna, he was practically in tears. She hugged him tightly and kissed his cheek, promising him free drinks for life at the cafe.

His superiors organized the other security personnel quickly, helping maintain order with the marines. They tried to convince Ander to relax and stand down but he refused, helping out until he practically couldn't stand. When he and his colleagues sat down for a hot meal, he nearly cried again and the thought of a warm bed made his limbs feel heavy.

The administrator himself, Kayle Ci'dala, visited while they were eating and took Ander aside. "You've done a brave thing and I want to personally thank you."

"It's okay…" Ander couldn't handle much more in the way of appreciation. "Really, I'm glad to have helped."

"I've managed to get you a promotion and a pay increase…which is the least we can do. You've also earned yourself two weeks of paid leave, in addition to what you've already accrued." Ander began to protest but Kayle lifted his hand to stave it off. "You've given us our lives, my friend. The least we can do is repay you with some rest and relaxation."

"Then...thank you. I appreciate it."

"For now, I think you've earned yourself some real rest. Is there anything else we can do?"

Ander shook his head. "No, I've never felt more appreciated...not even when I was in the army. This has been amazing. I look forward to many more years of active service. Thanks again."

"Think nothing of it and enjoy your time off. You probably need it."

Ander returned to his dinner and accepted the congratulations of his peers. He thought about what he might do with his time off, where he might go and how he might spend it. His family was spread out so there was little point in going home but there were a few vacation spots not hit by the war which might be nice.

He considered asking Tierna if she wanted to go with him. His status as hero might just allow him to talk her superiors into letting her go for a little while. He hadn't found anyone to pursue romantically since leaving the military and it might be nice to enjoy a little feminine company for a change.

But first, he intended to sleep in his own bed for as long as his body wanted. After everything he went through and all the things he longed for, that was by far the most interesting to him and the most important. His friends insisted on a few drinks but afterward, he returned to his room and flopped on his mattress face first.

Sleep came quickly. The rest of his life would be along soon enough.

***

Seventeen hours after they took the station back, the Behemoth saw the last of their crew come back aboard the ship. They had successfully assisted the station personnel and brought them back up to one hundred percent operational status. Ulem was delivered and stored in the cargo bays. Now, all they had to do was get themselves back home.

Gray allowed them another shift to stow their gear, get some rest and prepare for the journey back. Jumps were quick but they taxed the crew and most of them needed a little downtime before they returned. He sat in his quarters going over the after action reports, impressed by how efficient everyone operated throughout the mission.

A knock on his door grabbed his attention and he called out for them to come in.

Clea stepped inside and closed the door behind her, leaning against the door frame. He smiled, gesturing for her to have a seat. She complied, sinking in as if she battled exhaustion of her own. "Do you want a drink?" He offered.

"Yes, please."

He poured them each a glass of bourbon. "You look like you've had a rough shift."

"We've been studying everything Thantis did to the station and tried to help the current computer technicians institute some better security." Clea sipped and rubbed her eyes. "It's not exactly easy. They were very behind the times and were a bit put out by our efforts."

"Change is never easy, even when it's become absolutely essential, right?"

"I guess." Clea shrugged. "But in any event, no one should be able to waltz in and take things over like that again. At least, not if they follow our processes. I think they will. The administrator was...well, understandably upset about what happened. Their head technical person is being let go and sent back to the capital in shame."

"Ouch...but I'm not surprised."

"Nor am I. After all this...it was close." Clea snapped her fingers. "Oh, I almost forgot. Repairs on the station were complete where the pirates ripped their way out of here."

"Good, I was wondering about that."

"Bastards did a serious number on that corridor. Apparently, their own ship was something of a death trap as a result. If the Aguna Spear hadn't stopped them, Engineer Higgins says their ship would've exploded during a jump. Apparently, when the pirates were told they were pretty unhappy with their pilot."

Gray smirked. "I bet. That's a rough situation. I'm sure they thought they'd escaped too."

"Indeed." Clea shook her head. "Anyway, I think that's all the juicy bits I've got to offer. Do you have any yourself?"

Gray nodded. "Yes, I sent a message of our success directly after we confirmed everything was okay. The council got back to me about two hours ago. They were quite pleased and Anthar Mei'Gora wanted to personally commend you on your performance. The bridge staff figured prominently and swimmingly in my report."

"Thank you." Clea frowned. "I…had hoped not to see that man for a while."

"Why's that?"

"The way he acted when I turned over my sister to him…I didn't much care for it." Clea shrugged. "But then again, he's just a politician…a military politician at that. Which means he's not particularly good at being subtle. I figure his bluntness made sense to him and he probably thought he was kind."

"Yes, I doubt he was trying to be cruel." Gray checked the tablet. "We're going to leave in a couple hours. Do you want to play a game while we wait? Or do you think you should get some rest first?"

"Oh, I've slept. I just look tired. I'm not actually. Maybe it's just mental fatigue. I'd hoped you'd want to play. I needed the distraction."

"Then I'm happy to oblige." Gray stood and gathered the chess board, setting it up between them. "Tell me something, how did you feel about Thantis's reasons for attacking the station? I know how you feel about your own family. What's your thought?"

"No tragedy is worth murdering innocent people," Clea replied. "I don't care what you've been through, it's simply wrong. Anyone who says otherwise is trying to justify their own poor behavior. I found him to be reprehensible and insane. That's the only way I can think of that a person would be able to do what he's done."

Gray nodded. "I wondered if that's what you'd say."

"You had a prediction?"

"Well, you know...Earth people value vengeance sometimes. Our entertainment glorifies it and as people watch, they vicariously live through the hero. They take pleasure in seeing people get their just desserts. I don't think that any human would consider themselves justified in doing what he was up to...but I see where he was coming from."

"Which doesn't mean you think it was okay..."

"Heavens, no. But he lost everything and the only way forward for him was to destroy the last thing he found cause to hate." Gray shrugged. "I guess for my part, I just need to know it makes sense. I hate when crime is totally random or chaotic. It makes it far scarier."

"I guess that's true. I'd like to think that kielans are beyond such horror...but Thantis reminded me we're not. No one is. Anyone can be pushed to do something bad."

"Right now, I'm going to push you to make your move." Gray gestured. "I'm giving you white."

"You hate it when I'm black." Clea smirked. "I think I've won our last six games when I started as black."

"Why do you think I'm turning the tables? Literally."

"Very well." Clea moved a pawn. "I will happily take up this challenge, Captain...and thoroughly enjoy trouncing you from a new angle."

"Don't get cocky," Gray warned, moving his own pawn. "I might've been thinking about this for a long time."

"Then I expect a great deal." Clea paused. "Thank you...for all that you've done for me as of late. For my career, my health...my personal life...I won't forget it. I promise you."

"That's what friends are for." Gray sipped his drink. "Now, get moving. I don't have all night and I need to take you down."

"Bring it on, sir. Bring it on."

Epilogue

The Behemoth received clearance to go from the station and headed out to deep space where they'd make their jump home. The Aguna Spear remained behind as protection until another vessel could arrive. They didn't trust their guidance systems so decided to do repairs and wait for backup.

Gray allowed Adam to take the shift off, committing to getting them home with secondary bridge staff. This allowed Redding, Timothy, Olly and Agatha all a chance to get some extended downtime. Considering their last two missions, he felt they deserved and needed it. Those he surrounded himself with at the moment, though green, were excited to get them back and he enjoyed their enthusiasm.

The station wished them a safe voyage as they moved out of range. He had the communication's officer send a message to Earth letting them know they were on their way. By the time it reached them, the Behemoth would be safely docked and transferring their cargo but Gray liked to be cautious.

Jumping could be unpredictable.

As he offered up his final order for the ship to depart the sector, he leaned back in his chair and enjoyed a moment of silence. He appreciated his post, his career and most of all his ship. It and all aboard exceeded his expectations time and again. Gray looked forward to many more years serving with them.

"We're ready to initiate the jump, sir."

Gray nodded. "Take us home please."

The weightlessness he'd come to find familiar gripped him, his stomach tightened, the ship shuttered...and the jump began, sending the hurtling off through the vastness of space.

Printed in Great Britain
by Amazon